I0664406

ADVANCE PRAISE

I HAVE READ, I believe, almost every book Robert Newton has written! This may well be one of the best, in terms of enjoying the topic and getting wrapped in the conversation Newton has created between his characters, James and Ann. The topic is one I daresay not a lot of writers would tackle, nor would they take the time to research a subject, this controversial, in such a short period of time—and be able to convert it to dialogue between two people who know each other well, which allows him to put a bit of levity into a difficult theme and take away a bit of the sting we should feel.

Newton has written on certain elements of this topic in several of his other books, but the tone is significantly different; less academic and more enjoyable somehow. I daresay a number of readers will quickly put the book down and call his facts fiction; others will feel the kind of awareness that builds a fear of sorts; and still others, like myself, will do the fact checking and come away knowing we have learned a few new things, and have had other questions clarified and validated.

What Newton does not do is blatantly slam any of the personages mentioned throughout the book. Certainly he has his personal opinions, and in his well-known characters allows them to surface; however, I didn't find a single fact mentioned in the story without substance and substantiation. The delivery of which is softened considerably with the interchange between the characters.

The best part of *A Nation of Deceit* is the fact it is a soft entry into a topic critical to our nation. We must become more aware, take more responsibility for the amount of government control we embrace, and manage our lives in a manner that does not make us vulnerable for the "pickings" of events, actions, and controlling entities Newton reveals herein. In the wisdom of Aristotle, "The ultimate value of life depends upon awareness and the power of contemplation rather than upon mere survival."

~T. R. Stearns
EdS, Retired Superintendent of Schools

A NATION

OF

DECEIT

A Nation Deceived ~ A Nation Aggrieved
Finding A Solution ~ A New Evolution!

Copyright © 2016 by Robert J. Newton, J.D., N.D

Common Law Copyright, 4-22-16 by Dr. Robert J. Newton

All rights reserved. No part of this publication may be reproduced, distributed, or transmitted in any form or by any means, including photocopying, recording, or other electronic or mechanical methods, without the prior written permission of the publisher, except in the case of brief quotations embodied in critical reviews and certain other noncommercial uses permitted by copyright law. For permission requests, write to the publisher, addressed "Attention: Permissions Coordinator," at the address below.

Beyond the Bounds of Earth Publishing,

Entertainment and Education

Great Motivational Talks

A Nation of Deceit

ISBN-13: 978-0996137119 (Great Motivational Talks)
ISBN-10: 0996137114

Also available in digital (Kindle)

Dr. Robert J. Newton
20253 Evening Breeze Dr.
Walnut, California 91789

http://www.drrobertnewton.com/

Ordering Information:
Quantity sales. Special discounts are available on quantity purchases by corporations, associations, and others. For details, contact the publisher at the address above.

Printed in the United States of America
First Edition

14 13 12 11 10 / 10 9 8 7 6 5 4 3 2 1

DEDICATION

A Nation of Deceit is dedicated to every American citizen who is plagued by frustration, fear and despair about the tenor of the leaders of our great nation.

It is dedicated to

...the hope for a political and social culture driven by issues morally complex, yet driven by seemingly simple-minded hostility.

...my fellow Americans who question what has happened to what we believed made us the proud leaders of a free world.

...the disenfranchised and vulnerable who question whether our Nation can stand, or whether to embrace the reality we've lost it already.

In a time of universal deceit - telling the truth is a revolutionary act.

~ Unknown

TABLE OF CONTENTS

A Trail of Deceit Where Truth We Never Meet!

PREFACE

THIS IS MY eighth book, and actually given precedence over another half done. I really did not intend to write a book on this exact subject, having already finished *Planet of the Stupids: Bringing Back the Light of God to Planet Earth and a Paradise Found*, a cutting edge novel that shows what happens when countries are overtaken by socialism and Communism.

However, and this is a huge "however," what was happening in the Democrat and Republican presidential primaries disgusted me at a level I have rarely experienced in this lifetime. When a country is overtaken by systemic defamation... libel and slander... as a routine part of the electoral process, what happens is lies, distortions, things taken out of context, and outright fabricated evidence, which become accepted as a normal part of the "political process."

When political parties try to manipulate the primary results to get the candidate they want, in both the Republican and Democrat parties, in contravention to the will of the people, it makes the whole act of voting, basically redundant.

When rampant voting fraud skews the election results in a presidential race, voting becomes an exercise in futility.

Ultimately, because of the presidential primary and general election tactics by candidates, I decided to complete research about presidential elections at the beginning of the United States of America, and then bring a focus to recent times.

What I found did not surprise me!

Like a luminary, it showed an extremely deep level of defamation, a deliberate rigging of party conventions and outright voting fraud, meaning illegal voting by people not legally qualified to do so. So although this is a novel, the events shared herein, are factually true. Please join my characters, James and Ann, who surface from some of my previous books, including *The Hidden Codes of God*, *Beyond the Mists of Time: When Trees Ruled the Earth*, *In Search of the Body Immortal*, and *Planet of the Stupids*. There is a pattern with these characters in each of my novels as they sift through a lot of history; in this present story they lead us on a journey… a study of how we might do things differently in our presidential and other elections!

Dr. Robert J. Newton, J.D., N.D.

ACKNOWLEDGEMENTS

THIS BOOK IS for those people who are devoted to freedom and liberty. Some of you know as each day passes, your government takes away your liberties and freedoms through legislation and executive orders, and these things are in short supply, in a manner of speaking. One person who taught me about this was Robert Mueller, as he revealed an organization... a cabal... a cult... the Illuminati, whose main purpose is to enslave humanity like what occurred in The Dark Ages, and through every Communist government foisted upon humanity. This is done through compliant politicians and lobbyists with devious and hidden agendas. It is interesting, is it not, how these governments always collapse, but not before spreading their misery and inequity as they masterfully extinguish liberty and freedom, throughout a country.

Many of the issues I write about come from the *American Free Press* newspaper, *Judicial Watch*, and "The Pew Poll," "The Lou Dobbs Show," "The Shaun Hannity Show," "The Ledger," by Graham Ledger,

John Stossel, Victor Thorn, James Tucker, Michael Collins Piper, and "The Bill Reilly Show." I am indebted for their continual and fanatical search for the truth, which is well obscured in the mainline media outlets. I am indebted to my deceased wife, Charlette Ann Newton Smith, my current wife, Bertha Eloina Newton and my son, Charles Robert Newton… for their counsel and support in my writing and other endeavors. Indispensible in the creation of my many books, is my editor and literary coach, Anna Weber. She not only "polishes" my books, she assiduously fact checks them. So whether my books are novels or non-fiction, you can know they are factually correct.

"The truth is out there," as was the byline of one of my favorite TV shows, "The X-Files." I have found much truth in Kriya Kundalini Yoga, Tai Chi and Taoism, *The Yoga Sutras, The Bhagavad Gita, The Vedas, The Upanishads, The Ramayana,* and "The 72 Names of God," from "Exodus 14: 19-21 of *The Torah.* May we always remain connected to the Light, as per *Hey Resh Chet*, the 59th Name of God.

To that light,

Dr. Robert J. Newton, J.D., N.D.

A NATION

OF

DECEIT

A Nation Deceived ~ A Nation Aggrieved
Finding A Solution ~ A New Evolution!

by

ROBERT J NEWTON JD ND

CHAPTER I

HOW NOW, BOW WOW, HOLY COW...
OR NOT?

JAMES ALWAYS EXHIBITED a deeply idealistic streak, even from the early days of his youth. For sure, when he was growing up in the early 1950's, idealism was not considered a necessary or useful quality by which to differentiate and define one's self! Not only was James' idealism not understood by his peers—his playmates or schoolmates—neither was it understood by his schoolteachers, his Sunday school teachers or even his parents.

By the qualities and times he chose to incarnate on Planet Earth, James had already guaranteed he would be significantly different than anyone else. He, before his incarnation on Earth, did not consider the difficulties he was creating for himself by being born left handed and being incarnated on Halloween. He made the mistake of assuming his parents of choice, before his incarnation, both left-handed themselves, would cut him some slack and understand his Earth mission, which was restoring Earth to its Divine potential and archetype.

A type of love and caring indeed his parents did provide... yet they really could not comprehend how James was always a champion of the down trodden and those who were racially discriminated against. The discrimination James felt was not always portrayed in relation to one's skin color but also in regard to their nation of origin. as he personally witnessed two friends of his being harassed in elementary school because they were of German origin, in a time frame shortly after World

2

War II, and Adolph Hitler and the Nazis were fresh in everyone's mind. Unfortunately, James existed during a time when anyone German was assumed to sympathetic to Hitler and his Nazi Party, with very little thought being directed as to whether this was in fact true.

James readily embraced at an early age that his mission was to bring a political awakening in his country of incarnation—America—where candidates would be selected by their moral character, solutions to problems, and a deep, abiding caring for their constituents. This became a prelude to his spiritual awakening of humanity in general, beyond the confines of religion, and fostered by a highly ethical and principled nation of people, of which religion and spiritual values are a definite par. Anything less could not foster a climate where spiritual growth, a great respect for the Creator and the creations there from. Each was essential to foster, germinate and grow into something that would bear sweet and nourishing fruits! From James' perspective, most "fruits" on Earth were quite bitter, and such bitterness included more than just taste as it were!

Jumping forward, as the intervening time of James life, which was covered in *The Hidden Codes of God* scribed by Dr. Robert J. Newton... suffice it to say, James had many profound spiritual and sexual awakenings that are rarely experienced on planet Earth. He was blessed to have met his soul mate, Ann, at the end of his college days. James felt shaken—the proverbial being kicked in the head—when, much later in their relationship, his soul mate, lover and teacher, died a gruesome death in his arms. Recovery from such an experience is only achieved by becoming engrossed in consuming projects, be they work, something creative, or researching and learning new things. That is exactly what James did! He remotely viewed the scientific and esoteric aspects of immortality, as portrayed in several intriguing books: *In Search of the Body Immortal, Beyond the Mists of Time: When Trees Ruled the Earth*, and *The Immortality Prophesy*.

Remote viewing was a psychic ability James developed as he learned and practiced Kriya Kundalini Pranayam(a) breathing meditation from Kriya Kundalini Yoga. The extended breathing regimen James practiced produced altered states of consciousness produced by alpha, theta and upper delta brainwaves, like what people access when they use Cannabis, and in a higher amount, in the use of Ayahuasca, Psilocybin, LSD, etc. These brainwaves not only facilitated James' remote viewing, they also deeply developed other psychic abilities, including telepathy and pre-cognition. It was telepathy James used to communicate with his deceased wife, Ann, in the higher dimensions of Heaven. In fact, for what he contemplated, going back to the beginning of the history of the perceived great nation—the United States of America—both remote viewing and his ability to telepathically communicate with Ann would be crucial, as will become clear.

What James really wanted to investigate was the integrity of the various people who had been president of the United States; he was deeply aghast at what was occurring with the 2016 Republican and Democratic primaries. There was one candidate in the Republican primary contests, Donald Trump, billionaire developer, who although being rather uncouth and brash, was promoting a message of economic change by eliminating the abuses in free trade agreements like NAFTA, GATT, and TPP and uncontrolled immigration. Each was a major issue, both of which threatened the economic security of working, middle class Americans. as increasing numbers of jobs were eliminated by trans-national outsourcing and illegal alien workers who were willing to work for lower wages.

Well, "The Donald," as Trump is known, faced an onslaught of opposition from the Republican party officials, who coined him a misogynist, unpresidential, having no political experience in foreign affairs and economically uninformed; these things were also foisted about by their mouthpiece, who was tagged with the name, Ted Cruz, who used the disingenuous moniker, *TrusTed*.

A wolf in sheep's clothing, Cruz routinely used the Bible and the authority of the United States Constitution, to make his arguments, seemingly from a distant planet, to promote his candidacy. Yet, when his arguments were scrutinized, they could not meet the muster of factual accuracy or even the remotest tinges of truth. Many people found the rantings of Cruz, even more ironic as his last name in Spanish, cruz, means cross. His message was actually considered a blasphemy to Christianity itself, due to his endless untrue and fabricated statements. Additionally Ted Cruz was constantly extolling the virtues of his lawyer, wife, all the while obscuring the fact she was part of the Council on Foreign Relations, which is a front organization for the U.N. and Illuminati; viewing this travesty of truth made James stop and wonder if this trend of untrue grandiose statements, untruths, and manipulation were part of the history of presidential politics or something endemic to current times.

James' doubts of the honesty maintained in past presidential political campaigns was further stoked by the Democratic primary elections, where upstart Bernie "The Bern" Saunders, was challenging the existing Democratic party officials, represented by Hillary Clinton, who James had given the moniker, *Hillbilly.* In fact, Hillary had considerably more education than most hillbillies, but she could be deceptively dangerous and brutal in a most deceitful manner, like a moonshiner trying to protect his still. Clinton would stop at nothing to protect her many past misdeeds and misconduct, including making her enemies "disappear." Many of Clinton's dubious activities were pointed out by The Bern, including being funded with obscene amounts of money from banks, Wall Street brokerages, Monsanto's GMO (genetically modified organisms) foods, and questionable pharmaceutical companies. Hillbilly Hillary vehemently claimed such monies did not affect her decisions in the past and would not in the future. Only a fool would believe her assertion; almost everyone knew she would be beholden to these economic interests, indeed… to the detriment of the populace at large.

In spite of the controversial turnings, Clinton was winning the most primaries. Her success defied any type of logic, especially since a majority of the American people believed she was untrustworthy. Bernie pointed out that Hillary's sources of campaign funding were contrary to the best interests to the people, who needed higher wages and universal medical care/coverage.

Hillbilly Hillary, with her continual barrage of lies, seemed unlikely to be derailed by The Bern, despite widespread support from many segments of society, including the younger people of college age.

One thing James had been giving considerable thought, *I wonder if the computerized voting is being manipulated and skewed in favor of Hillary Clinton, in light of the fact that Hillbilly Hillary has such high negative perceptions as to her likeability and her proclivity to routinely lie about all manner of things.* James also thought about other similar disparities in voting history: *I remember when "The*

American Free Press" newspaper discovered in the 2000 elections, in fact Ozone Al Gore had won the exit polls in Ohio, Pennsylvania and Florida and would have won the election but for precinct computers being manually re-programmed.

As one thought followed another, James voiced his next concern, speaking to no one in particular, "Of course now, we know this can be done remotely, so considering Hillary's highly "unfavorable" rating, it is much easier to embrace this idea of computer vote tally manipulation."

Some time later James' research proved this to be true: Hacked emails from the Democratic National Committee (DNC) revealed an active campaign to prevent Sanders from winning the nomination... at all costs.

The information kept piling up; each new tidbit convinced James it was crucial to see whether political behaviors, rife with abject deceit and a pattern of deeply disingenuous propaganda were endemic to his time or it had slowly been cultivated over the history of America. Of course, in the distant past, there were no computers... James knew, however, to work through his quest he would

9

need specific things: the help of Ann, since she had done extensive research into some of the past American presidents, especially George Washington; his abilities of remote viewing, to look into the past and even the future, to see not only what happened on the third dimension Earth he inhabited, but also parallel Earth dimensions and higher aspects of Earth in the fourth and fifth dimension, existing in the quantum field, from quantum physics and quantum mechanics.

The way James always primed and honed his psychic abilities was using the Kriya Kundalini Yoga Pranayama(a), deep breathing mediation regimen he learned from Dr. Robert J. Newton. It helped him telepathically connect with Ann and zone in through his remote viewing. Poised for connection, James began to hone in on Ann's earthly picture, and sure enough, within short order, she made mental contact with him. A broad smile came over his face, which he tried unsuccessfully to hide, as James reunited with his soul mate of many lifetimes.

James was smiling; Ann made a goofy face and smiled at him, which just made him laugh loudly and for quite a time. Ann mentally "asked" him,

"Who were you expecting, Mr. Smarty Pants... the man who wants to open many cans of smelly worms? You really might not like what we uncover in our chronicles back into past presidential races! In fact, knowing how idealistic you are—in a most uncompromising manner—I am positive you will not."

"Indeed, I am sure I will not like it, Ann, and for sure you are right because I am intuiting a pattern of presidential candidate lying, propaganda and misdeeds that the populace is oblivious to or at least, unaware of," James replied, in a somewhat sardonic manner. "My feeling is I am not the only one who is completely disillusioned by the sliminess of politics. So far, the only U.S. president I know of who has not been involved in the devolved process of winning at all costs, is General George Washington and I know that because I know you read almost every book ever published about Washington. I wonder if we will find anyone else?"

"Indeed! I did read every book I could find about George Washington and you might be surprised by the many things I learned, James," Ann rejoined in an authoritative manner. "The thing about him was he really did not want to be president, or even the commanding general of the Continental Army fighting for the independence of the U.S. from England. Actually, it was by wide acclaim, among the political elite and the populace at large that George Washington was the best person qualified to be president. Interestingly enough, a significant number of people wanted him to be their king. So you see, James, if we look at the king suggestion, I would warrant that would make Washington the most trusted president of all time. He was also the most organized person to hold the position and should be given credit for creating the functional blue print by which the United States operated. Just consider the Treasury of the United States, as an example, until the perversion of recent times. I am afraid, thereafter, mudslinging, 'dirty tricks," and lying became de riguer in presidential politics."

Ann continued her dialogue and noted, "After Washington served his two terms as president, by unanimous vote both times, I might remind you... John Adams, Washington's vice president, ran for president and resorted to calling his opponent, Washington's Secretary of State, Thomas Jefferson, an atheist, low life, half breed, and sired by a mulatto father. Fast forward, James, to the 1796 presidential campaign, where Jefferson, playing the in-kind game, boldly accused Adams of being a "monarchist" who wanted to be king and was a fool and hypocrite, to wit. So here, we see the beginning of the descent into slimy political practices that have only become slimier as things slither down a precipitous slope, as we will see in succeeding presidential campaigns, with only a short interlude or two.

It was as though Ann was giving James time to absorb her conversation, and when he didn't respond, she offered her opinion on the whole of it. "Don't you agree, James, the outcome of these lies and distortions was Adams taking the lead and winning the 1792 presidential election? You could posture he had already an advantage, since he was Washington's vice president, whereas Jefferson was Washington's secretary of state and Alexander Hamilton was Secretary of the Treasury. Adams cast twenty-four tie-breaking votes on legislation that came from his Congress. He also rammed five 'Alien and Sedition Acts' through Congress—acts designed to control free speech and which made Adams very unpopular, especially with Jefferson."

As Ann continued, she shared more of her awareness with James. "So it is kind of a type of

13

karmic justice that Jefferson really turned up his propaganda machine, with an incessant barrage of fabrications against Adams to win the presidential election of 1800. It is more than ironic that Adams and Jefferson were in fact close friends."

James could hear the poignancy in Ann's message as she said, "I have to wonder, however, James, is this what friends do to friends, because such behavior seems to me a huge shift from a more ethical presidential behavior, which was the cornerstone of Washington's two presidential terms."

"How, wow, brown cow!" James blurted out, "So you are telling me that Adams was actually the responsible party for something similar to the most obnoxious 'Patriot Act' and the NDAA? In retrospect, we can validate our Constitution and the Bill of Rights, were already being undermined."

A quiet pause and James carried on his end of the conversation as his mind absorbed the message Ann had to share. "Ann, do I remember you telling me about Washington's farewell speech when he was leaving office and declaring there were forces in play that were already undermining the Union?"

"Yes, James," Ann intently responded. "And what you mention is not only disconcerting but also 'telling' as to the many dilutions and restrictions placed on the most perfect governmental and political structure ever created, in my personal opinion and that of many political scientists. Yet it is not hard to observe—if your fix your gaze on this subject—the Constitution was never really given a chance to be successful, as bankers put their energy into destroying it... slowly like a river wears down the stones therein; slowly eroding the foundational governments of America.

Ann paused, taking time to pull from her memory the many things she had read. The next President she discussed was Jefferson. "Certainly, I will point out more things, but this time about Jefferson. He had several accomplishments, which you shared with me previously. First, he pushed the Louisiana Purchase to buy a huge tract of land from France. Additionally, he set up the grid work/layout of Washington D.C. with Masonic/Hermetic/sacred geometries... the same geometric forms found on the atomic level of creation, revealed in Valery P. Kondratov's, *Geometry of a Uniform Field,* many of which are accomplished through the use of bisected diagonal streets you find in D.C.

"Yes," James laughingly responded, "I remember seeing this in some of my remote viewing sessions when I am afforded altered states of consciousness to view the past or the future. I can't tell you how excited I am sometimes to find the viewing in other timelines known as parallel Earth's and higher dimension Earth's functioning in the fourth and fifth dimension. I should add, those diagonal streets in D.C. can be confusing at times, but apparently not to Jefferson, ha-ha!"

"Indeed you have, James," Ann rejoined, "as you well relayed in *Planet of the Stupids: Bringing the Light of God to Planet Earth—With a Paradise Found*, there are all these different permutations of Earth, that are often discussed in Quantum Mechanics; and I bet you have seen some very interesting things in these realms, yes?"

"Undoubtedly I have, Ann, but let's stick to my permutation of this third dimension Earth, as we examine this timeline first," James authoritatively replied. "So I what I do know was Thomas Jefferson resorted to more mudslinging in his presidential race with Adams in 1800, even going so far as to hire a professional writer to script and dispense many scurrilous things about the then-standing president. The result of Jefferson's actions was that he unseated Adams and became president for two terms. Subsequently, his best friend and fellow Mason, James Madison, followed him into the presidency. Now it cannot be denied that Jefferson accomplished many other useful things for the U.S.; he not only created the University of Virginia but was instrumental in developing institutionalized libertarian principles in government, which were a stark contradistinction to the Federalist/monarchist tendencies of Alexander Hamilton, who believed in strong governmental control over things."

James seemed to have done his own in-depth reading of these early leaders, and continued to share his knowledge with Ann. "Anyway, with Madison, we find just how significant were his pre-presidential accomplishments... including being a party to the drafting of *The Federalist Papers*, the *U.S. Constitution*, and *The Bill of Rights*. A busy, and forward thinking President, Madison, with the aid of Thomas Jefferson, also created the Democratic-Republican Party, extended the charter of the U.S. Bank so funds could be raised for the War of 1812... and of course was president during the war itself."

Mentally stimulating, this conversation with Ann gave James pause for deep thoughts on the matter, and after a moment he pointed out, "We must not forget 'The War of 1812' was a portrayed as a battle, but that designation was not assigned before the British invaders burned Washington D.C. to the ground! Madison also signed 'Macon's Bill #2,' which re-established trade again between the France and England with the United States."

James suppressed his usual funny demeanor as he chatted on with Ann, moving their conversation through the annals of US History. "Now we get into more disgusting slime in the 1824 presidential campaign, as John Quincy Adams, son of former president John Adams, hired a less than scrupulous writer to trick Andrew Jackson's wife into revealing personal information about herself. Naive at best, she had no way of knowing the writer was searching for dirt, and revealed how she left her physically abusive husband and married Jackson, before her divorce was final. The writer wrote the piece and proclaimed Jackson's wife was an adulterer. Jackson challenged him to a duel that ended in the writer's death."

James stopped for a much-needed breath, as he realized the excitement of the conversation almost made him for get to do so! "Is it little wonder Jackson countered Adams was an elitist pimp? In fact, Adams was actually Harvard educated, from an aristocratic family of sorts and it was never proven he was a pimp. The tactic achieved Adams' goal; he won the popular vote. However, when he discovered he had no plurality in the Electoral College he bribed Henry Clay with the position of Secretary of State. The intention was for Clay to deliver the electoral votes he accrued as a third party candidate in the election. Clay accepted Adams offer and provided the needed majority. I really don't know if this was the first use of the exchanging of political favor for a federal government cabinet position, but it certainly, at least, is an early use of the tactic."

"James, I must say that is more than interesting, actually fascinating," Ann responded in amazement at what he shared. "In fact, if I remember correctly from my reading, I learned Jackson used a common folks approach in the next election and even talked about himself being an illiterate general and war hero, who defeated the Indians and the English in two important separate battles in the War of 1812. Not to be bested, Adams countered, and accurately so, that Jackson had one of his own soldiers court marshaled and executed for spreading discontent through his war camp. Stop and think about it, James! So Jackson wins the election, but what kind of person would execute any of his soldiers for expressing his dislike about how things were going? I think I am ok with throwing him in the brig; that would be appropriate, but death?

"I would have to agree with you, *mon amour*, Jackson's actions were refrickingdiculous!" James was sarcastic in his proclamation and unceasing in his comments, added, "And I am finding that going through the chronicles of presidential campaigns is leaving a most disagreeable taste in my mouth. In my remote viewing sojourns, I have seen a parallel Earth avoid this mudsling template of presidential politics and another higher dimensioned Earth completely avoid the scourge of an established government. I hope we get to talk about that at a later time, Ann."

Nary a moment passed before Ann excitedly proclaimed, "Please, please reveal what you have seen and learned, James, and yes, let's definitely talk about this."

"Yes I will 'please, please' you, as it were, Ann, but I want to get to more of the mudsling and mud wrestling of the third dimension Earth of *mua*! I also want to dwell upon some misconceptions that have been propagated by incessant propaganda."

CHAPTER II

A NEW LOOK AT THE CLAIMS OF A CHRISTIAN NATION… AND A LOT MORE!

JAMES WAS ALWAYS most intent about things being factually correct! In light of this he shared with Ann, "The idea is always proffered and promulgated by conservative Republicans today… the United States is a country founded upon Christian principles. As you well know Ann, I certainly hold no argument with Christian principles, but I do contend if you mix them with government and create a theocracy, the only people who benefit from this are the theocrats, the religious authorities, who always are ready to impose their brand of 'truth' upon any and all citizens, whether they want such or not."

Stopping to consider his next statement, James then noted to Ann, "The present government in Iran, controlled by the mullahs/clerics, should be enough example to prove my point, but let's look at what the U.S. Constitution and court decisions and legislation says on this issue!"

James intently expounded on his points, "The Treaty of Malta, Article 11, states, *the government of the United States of America, in no sense, is founded upon the Christian religion...*" This treaty was drafted by the highly revered President George Washington, signed by his successor, President John Adams and ratified by the U.S. Senate. Yet, there is much, much more!"

"Realize further, Ann, and I know you most likely know all this from your research on George Washington... not only was he a Mason but so were his very close friends, Thomas Jefferson and James Madison. Now Madison, as we're both aware was the father of the U.S. Constitution and co-father of the Federalist Papers. What, then, do you suppose we have here?"

James didn't expect or allow Ann to respond, but continued with his thoughts. "With these men as guiding and founding personages, whom we know were part of the Fredericksburg Masonic Lodge, and knowing the Masonic creed as bound by high spiritual principles but no specific religion or dogma... do we, Ann, find specific things in the U.S. Constitution and the First Amendment which reinforce their foundation?"

"First, the First Amendment says, *Congress shall make no law respecting an establishment of religion, or prohibiting the free exercise thereof.* Secondly, the U.S. Constitution says, *No religious test will ever be required as a qualification for any office or public trust.* So, I have to tell you, Ann, when I hear any presidential or legislative candidate telling me, we are a Christian nation, and I could specifically refer to Ted Cruz, it becomes a situation of pukesville for me. It turns my stomach, it irritates and offends my mental acuity because Cruz is always boasting that he has tried all these cases before the U.S. Supreme Court and he is an expert in constitutional law! Do you blame me to think he is beyond delusional and more in the realm extreme ignorance since he either cannot or did not read the Constitution? Or does he just have an agenda to create a theocracy and the nasty miasmas and foreboding consequences there from?"

James gave way to his emotions and spoke once again, "Then we have the issue of Cruz using *The Holy Bible,* to add substance and authority to his words. We need to have a higher bar… a more exacting standard! Why do we as a people, tolerate such people as our prospective leaders?" It goes without saying James' last unspoken thought was, *Is it all to promote a 'pork barrel' favor to the fundamentalist Christian voters?*

"Ouch! Tell me how you really feel about Ted Cruz, Mr. Smarty Pants," Ann laughingly responded. "I can tell you are offended by the foul stench of his words and as a Scorpio, I know when people are disingenuous or ply a diabolical agenda, you cannot —no—will not just sit back and ignore such and rationalize it as just being a part of politics. I do understand you would naturally feel this is just more evidence for your point that governments are inherently oppressive, just by their dysfunctional need to *govern*, which means to *control* in Latin, and *ment*, which translates from *mind* in Latin. The natural reaction is to see the goal of government is to control our minds... but why?"

"The greater question, James, might be, "Is this how a democratic republic should be constituted... mind control? What think ye, O Smart One, of the smart pants?"

"Well, we will have to investigate and come to a conclusion about that, Ann." With circumspection, James further replied, "I do know there was a good president in Libya who was assassinated by U.S. government backed black-op forces and/or private mercenaries. You probably remember Mohmmar Kaddafi and, how in a hacked email video, Hillary Clinton bragged about how he was killed. I can only believe history will show there was never a leader in the history of Earth, who treated his people better. He provided free college education, universal health care and low interest loans so his people could afford to buy their homes. He had a large system of canals constructed so as to bring the desert into being a place to grow crops. No U.S. President has done this for his people, not even George Washington! I guess we might have to just console ourselves at least Washington knew and even proclaimed that as *people became more democratic, they would thrive commensurately with the degree to which this occurred.*"

"Is our charge, Ann, to address this perspective, and embrace the reality it tells why we no longer have a prosperous populace in America—because the vestiges of democracy have disappeared at a terrifying speed?" James then carefully emphasized, "And I know you know this in most part, the Masonic order is based on ancient Hermetic teachings as expounded upon in Manly P. Hall's,

Wisdom of the Ages. Now you know Ann, Christianity does not really fit into the esoteric Hermetic knowledge, although it has a deep reverence for God. So it might be more accurate to say the U.S. is a God-based country rather than Christian based entity. Do we look deeper at what these presidents and their parties showed us? Do we question their accuracy that we are tied to and led by neither Christ nor God, because their actions are just to antithetical to either? The one exception we have to accept is George Washington, who by the way, had no political party and was guided by the Hermetic, Masonic Order. So right away, Ann, each speaks volumes for incriminating evidence stacking up against our political parties!"

"Go figure," Ann disgustedly retorted. "The way these things are twisted around by political parties and politicians is most disagreeable and disgusting. This is why I have always been so enamored with George Washington, and now with your research, you can finally understand my effusive praise for him. I looked at some of the other presidents and their actions appalled and repulsed me, other than perhaps James Madison, James Monroe, and Harry Truman."

"Well, that is true and clearly conveyed is your message, Ann," James observed. "This appears to be one of those *duh* moments; it seems only duhlicious as to Washington, but we should investigate things further just to see if we can uncover just one more honest presidential candidate or political message. I guess we should examine James Madison since you have found little fault in him. The one thing I did find is Madison was selected by the congressional caucus of the Democratic-Republican party. However, then Vice President, Charles Coteswort, and British Ambassador, James Monroe, objected vociferously to this decision. Do you not feel at its essence, the decision held many elements of secrecy and sliminess attached to a back room deal, at least with respect to allowing citizen participation in the governing process? Yet, I can find no wrong doing attributed to Madison himself, suggesting there might have been an indirect political trick attributed to Madison through the congressional caucus, but not overtly, nor directly, against his opponent. If I think back on it, it appears to me most certainly,

Jefferson must have done considerable arm-twisting to get his friend, Madison, into a position to be elected president. A position I must remind you, left Madison to deal with the War of 1812, where the British were trying to conquer the land we had bought from France via "The Louisiana Purchase." Did you know, Jefferson initially undertook all this, because America refused to knuckle under to the Rothschild Bank, which then controlled the British monarchy and harbored the same designs on the United States? Many citizens thought this land acquisition was unnecessary and a real folly. Yet, what would the U.S. be without it today? Most likely a fractured and disjointed country! If France still owned Louisiana and the other areas, we might be eating a lot more croissants and baguettes than we do now, and maybe even more escargot, ha-ha! So in light of this, let's move on and who was the next president, Ann!"

"Ha-ha, nice lead in, James," Ann replied as she responded to his laughter. "Of course you know it was James Monroe, who in 1816 ran almost unopposed in that election! We are reminded William Crawford from Madison's Democratic-

Republican Party ran an nominal primary campaign against him; however, surprise, surprise, once again we find no real dirty tricks, foul play or slander involved in Monroe's presidential primary or general election. Monroe studied law under Thomas Jefferson and was befriended by him; we can assume that relationship influenced Monroe's outlook on politics."

Ann's discourse on Monroe continued, "The thing that James Monroe is most known for is *The Monroe Doctrine*, which basically put Europe on notice that the United States of America would not tolerate the meddling of European countries in the affairs and territories surrounding the original thirteen states. These thirteen states soon became fourteen, as Monroe pushed for the ratification of the state of Missouri. Monroe both supported and ratified the purchase of Florida from Spain, in which vice president, John Quincy Adams, was involved. He also had Adams negotiate *The Treaty of 1818* with Britain, which gave the U.S. rights to ports on the west coast of North America, known as "The Oregon Agreement." Think about this, James… a document, which was an important development that aided in the westward expansion of our United States!"

As Ann paused for a few moments, James revealed his understanding of Monroe, stating, "Probably no president was better prepared to be president than James Monroe. Consider his accomplishments: he was a Virginia legislator and governor, a diplomat, Ambassador to France, Secretary of State and Secretary of War, but never vice president. It is also strange that Monroe was not a Mason, since his mentor was Thomas Jefferson, who was deeply involved in the Fredericksburg Masonic Lodge. Monroe was even criticized as being an atheist, although his family followed the Church of England and he personally attended Episcopal Churches. Although he was not considered highly religious, he did say a few things related to Divine Providence."

"The real point here, Ann, is that once again we take this into its proper perspective. We recognize that even though Monroe belonged loosely to a Christian denomination, he, like his presidential predecessors, refused to bring Christian beliefs into the operational forefront of the United States government. Oh, how I long for such wisdom! Not due to any dislike of Christianity but rather because theocracy never really fosters liberty but rather a forced agenda upon the populace, something our presidential Masonic forefathers would never do. In retrospect, we must at least question how most certainly the clerics/mullahs in Iran have managed to do quite well, in their Muslim theocracy... at least for themselves!"

Now on a roll, James sustained his thought, " But don't think things have turned around re the murky dealings of presidential politics between Jefferson and Adams! After Monroe's two terms, we just covered, we see how down and dirty John Quincy Adams, the son of President John Adams, and General Andrew Stonewall Jackson would get during their presidential general election."

Ann asserted, quite as a matter of fact, "There were many loathsome acts related to this election! Maybe, in the case of John Quincy Adams, the proclivity to use slander and innuendo came from his presidential father, John Adams?"

"Indeed you could be right, Ann," James agreed, "but I am just wondering how many people know the Democrat and Republican parties were one and the same thing in their original permutation as the Democratic-Republican Party? Do I digress? Well, I guess it is more important to dwell on J.Q. Adams and Jackson, so let's get ready to rumble... or at least for a rumba, with some new dance steps, as well, ha-ha!"

"Ok, Ann, now we get back to the nasty politics of Jefferson and Adams, more specifically John Adams," James wryly commented. "I think you indirectly alluded before, Ann, John Adams DNA must have been transferred to his son and presidential candidate, John Quincy Adams! I know many people will probably roll their eyes when they hear this but... it has been shown that mother mice do in fact transfer their genes to their progeny. This was well conveyed in *both In Search of the Body Immortal: Let the Journey Begin* and Newton's *The Immortality Prophesy.* Each discussed how our DNA is a binary pairs computer code, as revealed in Dr. Hubert Yockey's, *Information Theory, Evolution and the Origins of Man.* It is this computer code aspect of DNA that allows information to be transferred from parents to progeny. Maybe this is summed up in the saying, *The apple doesn't fall far from the tree.*"

And James continued his discourse with Ann, saying, "We covered this before but it is important to drive home this point of political sliminess used by John Quincy Adams as he relentlessly slandered and belittled both Andrew Jackson, his presidential opponent, and Jackson's wife, Rachael, as well. Just to recap the story, Adams paid a reporter to befriend her and she revealed many things about her past with a physically abusive husband, who she left in favor of Jackson. The reporter wrote an article revealing this and called Jackson's wife an adulterer and a prostitute. I am happy to say such allegations are not handled in the same manner today! Jackson challenged the reporter to a duel and shot the reporter and lost the election as Adams planned."

"Other barbs were thrown as well, Adams claimed that Andrew Jackson was of mulatto origin, which seemed to be an often-used slander used between political opponents. Thinking back on our conversation, we have to consider the factually correct statement Jackson had one of his soldiers shot for creating disharmony in a military camp under his command, during the War of 1812. What this says to me, Ann, is the existence of slime and grime rife in presidential and other politics, and it really doesn't much matter what your DNA may be,

"Jackson's minions even accused Adams of not wearing underwear and going to church barefoot," James relayed in a state of disbelief as to the relevance to an election! "These seem rather small, barbed insults by today's standards but apparently were significant *faux pas*, in times past. We already discussed Adams' qualifications as president, but find Henry Clay the most determined candidate... followed closely by William H. Crawford, as another contender in this crowded presidential field. Both of these other candidates, had more experience than Jackson and both also received some popular votes in the Electoral College, as well."

"These factors certainly predicated the decision of who would be president to the House of

Representatives, because there was no majority victor in the Electoral College. In the House of Representatives, there was a lot of deal making and political favors being dispensed in order to become president. It bears repeating, the promises Adams is known to have made were to allow one of Clay's relatives to remain on the judicial bench and make Clay Secretary of State, in exchange for throwing his support to Adams.

"Yes, James, I wondered why you cycled this all back to Adams and Jackson," Ann said after taking in James' long discourse. "At the end of all this finagling, John Quincy Adams was selected as president and held one term after the 1824 election, but all the while, Andrew Jackson was plotting his revenge. Nevertheless, Adams signed *The Treaty of Abomination*, a necessary protection for American manufacturers from increasing foreign competition. The flipside to the treaty is that it forced people and companies pay more for manufactured goods."

"I don't know about you, I fervently believe it was a good and needed tradeoff to save American jobs, which is certainly necessary today, more than ever. Adams also pushed the building of more roads, canals, and schools and colleges and should be given due credit for creating the Second Bank of the United States."

Ann entered the conversation again, asking James, "Were you aware Jackson was upset Adams named William Clay as his Secretary of State, and Adams was perhaps not fully aware of Clay's deliberation; he believed that position would give him a strong foundation from which to run for president after Adams served his terms?"

"I consider just how our Nation was changed, by the manner in which Jackson reacted to his anger; he convinced Martin Van Buren to create a new political alliance from the Democratic Republican Party and new factions and it was from the platform of this party, the Democratic Party, that Jackson was later able to win the presidency."

"Can you believe the ugliness of human nature when Jackson focused his campaign on Adams' sharing one of his slaves when he was a Minister in Russia with the Czar who exploited her with his sexual aspirations and desire? Adams was further attacked for his royalist tendencies stemming from nothing other than his admiration for the many lighthouses built in Europe. It is well known that General Andrew Stonewall Jackson fought the Red Coat soldiers in the War of 1812 and passionately hated anything British—virtually anything from Europe for that matter. Should we question his preferences because he was not highly educated or cultured, for that matter?"

Taking Ann somewhat by surprise at his emphatic response, "Well, Ann, we have just to revisit the 1828 presidential contest. Jackson was again attacked for his marriage to his wife, Rachael, which had to be re-consummated since her divorce was not final from her physically abusive husband. For his actions, Jackson was actually labeled by some as anti-Christian and deemed not fit to lead a Christian country. Rachael was again painted as an adulterer and prostitute. Never to leave a stone unturned, Jackson's naysayers also denigrated him for his harsh behavior toward his troops when he was a general and his proclivity to settle disputes through dueling. During his candidacy, Jackson was labeled as a slave *trader*, but not for having slaves on his plantation."

"Isn't it interesting to discover exactly how the Christian designation of the origins of the U.S. were being bandied about in contradistinction to it actual Masonic origins? It is unfortunate for our Nation how people like to manipulate things as they want them to be, as opposed to what they actually were intended. This might lead us to conclude myriad politically motivated hidden agendas are not only part of presidential politics but something coming from the common citizenry, as well."

"In the election in point," James confidently asserted, "the influence of Jefferson's support of Jackson, before he died in 1826, helped Jackson win the election in a landslide in the Electoral College. Life seems to play a balancing act, and the victory for Jackson was extremely bitter because his wife, Rachael, died a few days after Jackson's victory. She had suffered stomach problems during the entire presidential campaign. We might ask, 'Were these stomach irregularities due to Rachael being unable to 'digest' the nastiness, outright slimy actions, and slanderous behavior during the entire presidential campaign?'"

"You know, James, as far out and outrageous, as it were, this might seem to others, the emotional-physical sickness connection is well chronicled in multiple publications, such as Louise L Hay's book, *You Can Heal Your Body* and in Dr. Robert J. Newton's book, *A Map to Healing and Your Essential Divinity Through Theta Consciousness*. In fact, I have experienced digestive problems when there are things that do not sit well with me, likewise!"

"Undoubtedly, Ann,'" James forthrightly replied, with an earnest tinge in his voice, "we have revealed some real truths as to the emotional-physical ailment syndrome and as it also relates to me personally. The body will always mirror the emotional state of the person inhabiting that body. Unfortunately, Ann, this relates to literally everyone on planet Earth, and most likely the Cosmos, as well. Let us, however, steer ourselves back to the achievements of President Andrew Jackson, because we still have so many other presidential contests to examine."

"We look now at how Jackson dismantled the Second Bank of the United States and forced the relocation of Indian tribes west of the Mississippi River. I guess this must have been easy for him, being an U.S. Army General, through the Indian Removal Act, but was one of many inequitable things that would happen to our Nation's Native Americans in the following years. Jackson overruled the *South Carolina Nullification Resolution*, which subsequently allowed this state to disregard any federal legislation related to tariffs. He also was the only president of completely pay off the national debt—despite the claims of President Bill Clinton! Additionally, Jackson negotiated a trade agreement with the British West Indies."

"Ann, we have to digest all this! What exactly did Jackson do in addition to the obvious screwing over the Indians? It is also pretty obvious Jackson strengthened the powers of the president and the presidential spoilage system, all in order to reward his supporters. I personally find both of these actions far from being noble but... what choices did we have? It should be back noted that Henry Clay actually got his chance to run for president in 1832,

but lost in another all too common nasty and slan
derous presidential contest."

"We know Martin Van Buren followed Jackson
into office—as a Democrat—as was Jackson," James
verified. "In fact, he won by a considerable vote over
the closest of three other opponents: Whig Party
candidate, William Henry Harrison. The ultimate
idea was to control the outcome by having the other
two Whig candidates, William Henry Lawson and
Daniel Webster, siphon votes away from Van Buren
so there *could not* be an Electoral College Majority
and the Whigs would decide the election in the Whig
controlled U.S. House of Representatives."

"Although it didn't work as expected, I think,
Ann, there is a lesson to be learned here: it shows
just to what lengths one political party will go to
stop the other… irrespective of the best interests of
the United States and its people. It is like the whole
thing is a competitive game. And this is the one that
boils me: actions of this nature further show us the
party establishments believe they are better able to
select their candidate than the people! Maybe that is
true, but if that is so, why cavalierly foist about the

idea of democracy when what we really might have is an autocracy?"

"You get where I'm coming from, don't you, Ann? I guess this is what initiated this conversation; it is so reminiscent of the "Stop Trump" movement of 2016, within the Republican elders such as the Bush family and The Romney's. What happened to Trump, overtly, yet unsuccessfully, occurred to Bernie Sanders, covertly, as Hillary Clinton and Democratic National Committee Chair, Debbie W. Shultz deliberately fomented a copycat campaign to keep Bernie Sanders from receiving the Democratic nomination. This was all revealed from "hacked" emails between and Shultz and Clinton, who in this case were successful. It is interesting what hacked emails, reveal, is it not, Ann?"

James continued as he shared Van Buren's endeavors, "You do know Ann, Van Buren followed Jackson's idea of decentralized banks but this could have led to a deep depression, many bank failures and massive unemployment. He tried to placate the Southern States by lowering tariffs and instituted selling bonds to finance the national debt. He also made sure Jackson's Indian relocation was carried out, leading to the Cherokee's 'Trail of Tears,' and other tribes being located west of the Mississippi. River. He also engendered diminished relations with Britain due to his foreign policies and denied Texas' attempt for statehood."

"Hey Mr. Smarty Pants," Ann replied with mock derisiveness! "It's me you are talking to; I know just how much you dislike the Electoral College. This seems to be another example of control issues where the rights of political parties trump—not tongue in cheek like the Donald Trump—the rights of the general electorate."

"Well, Ms. Smarty Pants, you know me only too well, but I am sure my pants are not the only smart thing about me... or at least I hope so," James laughed as he replied. "It is just so inequitable to have any condition where a candidate can lose the overall electoral count and yet still win the election in the Electoral College. Equally unjust as the way political parties are quick to use different unethical or marginally and/or dishonest strategies to win elections, just like the Whig Party did in the contest with Van Buren. This is really pukeadelic, no?"

"So, so true, James," Ann responded in a matter of fact manner. "You know, there are myriad people who believe their votes don't even matter. When you take a cold, hard look at these types of shenanigans and manipulating the vote tallies, you have to say their outlook is actually quite sane. But, rather than moan and groan about this, let's consider our next presidential election in the long list of our studies."

"I am not sure the next president, William Henry Harrison, is even worth considering since he died before one month after his inauguration," James conveyed. "Harrison was actually the first Whig Party candidate to be elected to president. He was the son of Constitution signer, Benjamin Harrison, and was a successful military leader who centered his campaign on these merits and his being a frontiersman, even though he was from a family of privilege. When Harrison served as governor of the combined territories of Illinois, Indiana, Michigan and Wisconsin, he was aggressive in the pursuit to push Indian populations from their territory to facilitate said areas being settled with white people.

"What a sweetheart," Ann sarcastically replied. "This certainly was not endemic only to Harrison but indeed, it is one of those 'dark blots' on the U.S. history and very embarrassing for many of us.

"Well", James laughingly replied, "it seems as though Harrison might have experienced his karma in spades, since he died from pneumonia before even a month into it had passed. What is the likelihood was to have no presidential legacy other than he was the first U. S. President to die in office. His unfortunate demise, however, does take us to his vice president, John Tyler, who filled the term of Harrison. Obviously Tyler didn't have to endure the anguishes of a campaign to become president of a one-term duration."

"Equally obvious is that during his term Tyler remained a busy beaver, where as President, he vetoed an obviously popular tariff bill, for which he was unsuccessfully impeached. He subsequently changed course and signed a tariff bill into law. The tariff was basically a north—south issue, with the industrial northern states in favor of tariffs and the southern states, who imported many things, from abroad, passionately anti-tariff."

James was really interested in what the default president, Tyler, accomplished. "You know, Ann," James continued, "Tyler's whole cabinet, other than Daniel Webster, resigned and returned to the Democrat Party because they mistakenly thought they could influence Tyler. Perhaps he did have the common man at heart when he chose to sign the *Log Cabin Bill*, which allowed settlers to buy U.S. government land at $1.25 per acre. Of course, if you think about it, most of this land became available only by removing the Indians from it and relocating them into reservations. For me, it is really difficult to see the legality and equity of an obscene policy that would continue for many more decades.

Ann had been listening to James but it was clear she was anxious to get into the discussion when she exclaimed, "You know, James, Tyler was a strict constitutionalist! He believed government powers were limited so he vetoed bills for a U.S. National Bank—two times. This stance certainly made him most unpopular with the Rothschild's international banking interests, as they privately owned these so-called federal or national banks."

"Following the Mexican-American War, Tyler signed off on the annexation of Texas, which had aligned itself with the South. It has been said that Tyler actually sowed the seeds of the Civil War through his actions, but who knows whether this is factually correct or just the opinions of people with an agenda?"

"It would seem Tyler's decision might have been the genesis of the Civil War, Ann," James rejoined. "There was a re-annexation of Texas during the presidential administration of James J. Polk and this really threw "gas on the fire" in the dispute between the North and the South. Actually, in this election, Martin Van Buren was presumed to have the inside track on being president for a second time. Yet the Democratic Party did not like his position on slavery, so it eschewed him. Now, Ann, don't you see how important it is we take notice that the party made this decision and not something decided in primaries... decided by party voters."

"Henry Clay was the Whig candidate—again decided by his party, and not through a primary decision—lost by 38,000 votes to Polk," James continued." This one of the closest elections in the history of the U.S., but what is most distressing... even disgusting... is how the democratic principles of electing candidates were circumvented."

"How ironic and yet telling!" Ann's sarcasm was loud and clear as she continued. "The whole system of elections and the electoral process is tainted. I think we might be better served by looking at solutions on Earth and, which we might find even on parallel Earths, James... what think ye?"

I cannot disagree with your assessment, Ann," James continued. "Certainly solutions were found to Earth problems in Dr. Newton's book, *Planet of the Stupids: Bringing the Light of God to Planet Earth— With a Paradise Found.* Some people have criticized this book as a wild stretch of the imagination, yet Quantum Physics and Quantum Mechanics have both posited, through *String Theory* and *Membrane Theory*, there are fourteen dimensions and parallel dimensions within them, as well, so... there is much more creation than has been shared in our religious texts and if that is our only source of information, we will most likely miss the larger picture and nuances of our world."

Rather than get sidetracked by another topic compelling to James, he said, "I would like to jump forward to James A. Garfield campaigning against Winfred S. Hancock in 1880. This was one of those all time dirty trick presidential campaigns where Hancock's campaign shared a letter allegedly from Garfield, saying he supported the importation of Chinese workers. The dirty trick easily worked to Garfield's disadvantage, because the populace at large was concerned about a growing Chinese populace displacing American workers in the labor force."

"You know, sometimes life steps in with a sense of what is fair and right, and when Garfield produced a copy of the letter he had written, in confidence, and its content and handwriting was compared unfavorably to the fake letter, the tide turned back in Garfield's favor and he narrowly won the election. Does this crap ever end, Ann?" Ann just rolled her eyes, shook her head back and forth and provided James a response with a quiet, wry smile.

As James switched course, he explained, "There is just such a low bar of ethical behavior in our presidents and aspiring presidents, as we have already seen, other than George Washington, Madison and Monroe. In this manner, during the Lincoln-Douglass Debates for an Illinois federal senate seat, Stephen Douglass slammed Abraham Lincoln for wanting to abolish slavery and for not supporting the Supreme Court case, *The Dred-Scott Decision*, which allowed the federal government to extend slavery into new territories and states, and that slaves could never be free or become citizens of the United States, at a time the majority of people probably favored such. So as a result, Douglass won the Senate seat."

"In 1860 John Bell and John Breckinridge also joined presidential candidates: Republican, Lincoln and Democrat, Stephen Douglass, in the race. Lincoln did not engage in any debates with other candidates and chose to meet with Electoral College delegates to influence their presidential choice. One highly dubious action on the part of Lincoln was his purchase of a German language newspaper. Lincoln actually thought he might be able to influence German immigrant voters if he could control the paper's editorials, and tilt their support toward him."

"The pervasiveness fills me with something far deeper than disappointment. It is frightening just how much political candidates are willing to lower their standards to win a contest, irrespective of how it smacks of a total lack of moral values, humanity, and truth. Obviously, Lincoln wanted to get even with Douglass from when he lost the senate race, and get even he did; the outcome of the election was never really in doubt!"

"Hey, James," Ann declared with a certain peevishness, "are you coming up for air or are you going to continue your Shakespearean soliloquy?"

James laughingly replied, "Out damn spot… out… a little bit in time, a little bit in time! Well maybe now that I have some time I can get the 'damn spot' out. I'm sensing you want to hear I am so sorry (Not!) for my effusive enthusiasm. Just remember much of it you instilled in me long ago when we were husband and wife. Actually, I forgot to tell you I swim with whales and I think you might know they only come up for air every three to four minutes. Anyway, any day...

"Wow, James," Ann acerbically exclaimed, "you sound like a politician yourself, with your long winded explanations, but since you are the 'whale whisperer,' what else would I expect, other than long winded?"

"Ha-ha, flaw, flaw," James responded. "Since you pointed out my flaws, I will point out Lincoln's flaws, even though he has been called "The Great Emancipator." Some historians, such as David Goldfield, in his book, *America Aflame: How a Nation was Created*, mentions how many countries had slavery but only the United States and Haiti ultimately eliminated the problems commensurate with slavery through a civil war. So, for as much I despise war, as you well know, because nothing any good really comes there from, I can never justify a war that pitted citizen against citizen, even though the idea of slavery is abhorrent for me. In Thomas Fleming's book, *A Disease of the Public Mind: A New Understanding of the Civil War*, he lays blame on the intransigence of both the northern and southern states as to what stimulated the war. Historian Bruce Ramsey, in his article, "Was the Civil War Really Necessary...," his perusal of historical records reveal the Republican's and Lincoln were 'more shrill than the Democrats on this issue, so I would say in their fervor, they unnecessarily fanned the flames of war.'"

"Now, I would further say," James continued in a decidedly direct manner, "it has often been stated W*Press* newspaper, bankers fan the flames of war, supporting both sides/all sides and profiting there from, regardless of who wins the war. In the article, "Jews Caused the Civil War," writer, Willie Martin points out his belief the Rothschild banking empire actually started the Civil War in 1837, when the federal bank's (really a Rothschild bank) charter expired."

"I wish you had read it, Ann! This article is very comprehensive, vis-a-vis the role bankers played in the Civil War. The Rothschild's, of Jewish origin, sent their agents to get a new 'national" bank chartered. This did not happen until 1861, after the southern depositors had withdrawn huge sums of money from northern banks. At the time, Lincoln was facing a huge shortfall of funds with which to finance a war. Actually, the Warburg's and the Rothschilds funded the northern (Union) war effort whereas the Rothschild's and the Vatican Bank gave funds in the cumulative amount of $2.5 million in funds, for the Confederate war efforts, without which the Confederate president, Jefferson Davis, could not have entered into a war."

"So prescient you are, my Whale Whisperer," Ann spoofingly addressed James. "And this is where things got interesting and something about Lincoln, who was also printing a northern currency, known as *Greenbacks*. Lincoln let it be known near the end of the Civil War he would be still be printing what was supposed to be just a temporary currency. Well, as you can imagine, James, this really pissed off the European banking families/sources who felt they were positioned to entirely control the U.S. money supply after the war. I'm sure they felt their anger was justified; they would have profited handsomely from the interest charged. Lincoln's course of action would prevent that from coming to fruition. It is pretty apparent that is when the European banking forces decided Lincoln must be assassinated... and assassinated he was, by acquaintance, John Wilkes Booth. Does that concept of Lincoln's assassination have enough intrigue for you James... er 'Whale Whisperer?'"

"Well, Ann, of the scrutinizing gaze," James blurted out, "certainly that is africkingmazing! I might possibly be having trouble deciding who is the more the bottom feeder... politicians and their lust for power or parasite banks who are caught up in a scheme of greed, with their onerous and usurious interest charges, which was $15 million on a loan of $2.5 million loan, for the Confederacy."

"But, I think I would like right now to shift our gaze to some other things. I know I am jumping over many other presidential elections but we really cannot skip over the Dewey-Truman election. It has been reported Truman was, in fact, overwhelmed when Franklin Delano Roosevelt (FDR) died and was thrust into the presidency. Truman concentrated on ending World War II, which ended not long after he ascended to the presidency."

'He was a man of humble means and a haberdasher by profession, so Truman was probably nattily dressed, yet not overly confident in meeting the public at the level the presidential campaigns had become, in contrast to the early presidential elections where most candidates never left their homes, due to the arduous logistics of moving around by horseback and/or carriage. Against high odds, Truman thought he could win the election. The competition was wide-ranging; Truman not only ran against Republican and New York Governor, Thomas Dewey, but also against States Rights Democratic candidate, Sen. Strom Thurmond and Henry Wallace. Truman won an election where he had started out far behind, having been blamed for the inflation in the economy and Democrats losing control of both houses of the legislature!"

"Well, well, well," joined in Ann, "how could I not be a fan, man? Truman went on a whistle stop train tour of the U.S. to promote his candidacy but Dewey, who had run against FDR in 1944 and lost, was expected to win by a landslide; the newspapers were so sure of this some of them made their headlines the night before, proclaiming Dewey's win. The thing for me that makes this election so special, other than Truman came almost out of nowhere to win, was how cleanly and ethically it was contested. Dewey might have been overly complacent about winning because of his initial huge lead and Truman did not stoop to lies nor libel or slander against Dewey to win the election. How rare, indeed, in the overall scheme of presidential and general politics, as well!"

"It just really blows me away, how a male and a female... well female angel, can see these events in a similar light, Ann; I'm your fan," James admiringly exclaimed. "Just in passing, let's chat a bit about the 1960 presidential race where John Kennedy played some dirty tricks on Richard Nixon, during their debates. Nixon asked Kennedy, just before their televised debate, 'Are you going to wear makeup?' Kennedy curtly responded, 'No I don't need it!' From this, Nixon decided not to use makeup, other than apply a little something on his own, which made him look pale."

"Now, I know you can appreciate that makeup makes almost everyone on TV look better. Although not horribly malicious in the act, Nixon was certainly betrayed by Kennedy, who actually did have makeup applied, by a professional makeup artist. Now you can say, whoop tee fricking doo, not something important to do, and yet it was. Nixon appeared to have dark shadows under his eyes, a *five o'clock shadow* and pale and dilapidated in his appearance, whereas Kennedy looked bright eyed and bushy tailed... vigorous and confident."

"The make-up trick was not the only reason Kennedy won a very close election... there were voting irregularities in Texas and Chicago that could have been challenged and swayed the election to Nixon, but after Vice President Nixon consulted with President Eisenhower, they agreed that being in the middle of a *cold war* with the Soviet Union, it would be better not to create chaos or uncertainty in the United States, where the American populace was already under great strain and uncertainty as to whether there would be a nuclear war with the Soviet Union."

"Certainly there was a lot of saber rattling on both sides, yet I remember going to bed at night, wondering if I would awake for another day on Earth or wind up atomized in a nuclear explosion of a bomb that was dropped from a plane or delivered via a nuclear missile warhead. I warrant saying few people in the sixties will ever forget about this experience! I know I **never will!**"

CHAPTER III

DO WE REALLY LIVE IN THE LAND OF THE FREE AND THE HOME OF THE BRAVE?

AFTER INTENTLY CONSIDERING James' words, Ann quietly replied, "It is just so interesting the illusions and myths people love to cling to and how people believe they live in the land of free and the brave...

and in liberty and fair and accurate voting tallies! Granted, we have quite a few brave people... it is just the free and liberty and honesty part that do not mesh with what really occurs in the U.S.! Nixon used his own dirty tricks against Hubert Humphrey, in the 1968 presidential race. He tied Humphrey to the failed Vietnam War policies of the sitting president, Lyndon Johnson. He also pounced upon the civil unrest occurring during Johnson's reign; blacks protesting their second class citizen status, segregation, and race discrimination."

"It could even be accurately said," James added, "the black populace often had an even lower than third class status, but that might not have been the fault of either Johnson or Humphrey, who, after all, created *The New Society* government programs that provided welfare benefits for all under-class people. Nixon did not much care about ethics or truth, and was fanatical and laser focused in his drive to become president at any cost... regardless the consequences of unethical behavior. In an ironic twist of fate, Nixon's penchant to disregard ethical standards led to the Watergate affair."

"I know you remember this, Ann; the scandal when Nixon's operatives, in a bold effort to collect incriminating evidence against McGovern in the 1972 presidential contest, broke into the Senator's campaign headquarters. Karma is so alive! Nixon won a successive term as president, but faced resignation when informants of Nixon's illegal behavior tipped off the investigative team of Bernstein and Woodward. His violation of integrity and abuse of power soon led to a congressional investigation and Nixon being impeached by the U.S. Congress. Nixon escaped the inevitable by resigning, and ceding the presidency to his vice president, Gerald Ford, who eventually pardoned Nixon of the impeachment."

"Little did Ford know that Jimmy Carter, who ran for president against him in 1976, would be eager to use that decision, plus a dismal plodding, sputtering economy to defeat his rival, Ford. Was this ethical? It seems borderline to me!"

"Borderline, schmorderline, all we see is an overt recycling of unethical behavior that just keeps reoccurring, much like a case of Herpes. Look at the analogy; a *disease* transferred from presidential candidate-to-candidate," Ann laughingly exclaimed, with sardonic undertones. "Additionally, James, we have to be open about something most people do not know. Nixon, long before he was elected president, contacted South Vietnamese President, Thieu, and asked him to pull out of the Paris Peace talks that were set up to create a peace between North and South Vietnam... with the promise Nixon would get Thieu a better deal for South Vietnam and he agreed to such. That decision would bite President Thieu in the ass and our nations soldiers, as well"

"I know you might be inclined to say, 'Who gives a *flying flapjack* about this technicality?' Yet it had at least two significant consequences we simply cannot dismiss. First, it extended the length of the Vietnam War, and made Humphrey and President Johnson both look like failures, regarding the Vietnam conflict. Secondly, and even worse, it meant more U.S. and South Vietnamese soldiers would be injured and killed... into the tens of thousands of our *free and brave* young men.

"OMG," James sardonically replied, "you know Ann because you were there with me! In our teens and early twenties, we really despised Richard Nixon, and our friend Rand and I called him 'Dickhead Nixon.' After all this time, and renewed awareness, it appears our assessment was much too kind; Nixon's disregard for the injuries and deaths suffered by soldiers, due to a deliberately extended war, reveals him as a cold hearted bastard—maybe even heartless."

"Now, we both know the acts of Ronald Reagan should not escape our gaze, Ann. Reagan, after suffering a Republican party primary defeat to President Ford in 1976, really upped his game against Carter in the 1980 presidential race. Reagan's prime ammunition, of course, was to fault Ford for the debacle where American embassy hostages were taken prisoner by a group of Iranian students who stormed the embassy. Reagan also pointed out that Carter was presiding over a faltering economy; he didn't note the same could be said about Nixon and Ford, as well, since it was a situation that had been *inherited.*"

"Well, that is groovy and all that, Mr. Whale Whisperer," Ann mocked James, "but even worse is the fact that, unknown to Carter, Reagan somehow got his hands on a copy President Carter's debate notes, before the televised debate between the two. When the debate occurred, Carter seemed baffled and confused; Reagan was always one step ahead of him, because he knew in advance everything Carter was going to discuss during their debates. In contrast to Carter's demeanor, Reagan projected confidence and a mastery of the debate issues, which turned the lead Carter had before the debate, into a rousing loss for him. I believe this occurred during the second of three debates Reagan had with Carter."

"So, Ann, did you know I met Ronald Reagan once at columnist, Jack Kilpatrick's house? I liked him and found him humble yet engaging. Yet, if I had known about the stealing of Carter's debate notes, I would have had problems even shaking his hand!"

"Hey, James of the whispering whales, I can see you really feel betrayed by Reagan's shenanigans and rightly so," Ann opined.

"Hey, Ann of the angelic scrutiny, there is even more," James sarcastically proclaimed. "As you will remember, President Reagan was shot in 1981 by John Hinckley and due to the investigative work of *The American Free Press* newspaper, we happen to know the Hinckley family was long time friends with the Bush clan. Now, you and I know, but very few other Americans do, that the Bush's are part of the oligarch elite, a cabal known as the as the Illuminati, comprised of the Bush clan, the Fords, Rockefeller's and the Mellon's; the Schwab's, Morgan's, Rothschild's, and the Warburg's; The Jesuit Catholic order (which is really a military order), the British Royal Family, and the Dutch Royal Family. Anyway, this naturally leads us to the fact President Reagan's policies were contrary to the goals and desires of the Illuminati. Further, we must consider whether this 'hit' on Reagan came via his Illuminati vice president, George W. Bush, which naturally leads to the deduction John Hinckley was aided and abetted in his assassination attempt on President Reagan. One credible observation from *The American Free Press* newspaper was how Ronald Reagan took a different tack than originally planned... a modified course of action after he was shot and came very close to dying... returning to health after several months' time."

After watching James present his case re the Reagan shooting, Ann laughingly declared, "Ohh, Eee, Ohh, Ahh, Ahh! James is a master of dancing around things, ha-ha, ha-ha! Why don't you just cut through all the drama and intrigue and just say the Illuminati, through their member, put a 'hit' out on Ronald Reagan?"

"Flew, flea, flu, ha-ha, what fun would that be, proclaimed the crow, caw, caw,!" James derisively laughed at Ann, and then exclaimed aloud, "That would be, like, no funsville, *mon amour!* Anyway, you must know I really do not want these Illuminati cultists crawling up Uranus... well, actually mine, ha!"

"Well, I guess the cat is out of the bag, eh, Ann!" Yet John Kennedy was also *disciplined...* actually, assassinated for incurring the wrath of the Cabal. Kennedy had planned to address the American people about two primary issues, after his fateful trip to Dallas. You see, two things in particular infuriated President Kennedy when he discovered them. The first was finding out the Federal Reserve Bank had no vestiges of U.S. Federal government and really was 'sticking it' to the government and American citizens."

"Secondly, Kennedy found out Israel had nuclear weapons in large numbers, despite the Jewish state proclaiming otherwise, even though "Jane's" defensive statistics indicate Israel is the fourth or fifth highest in the number of nuclear weapons; it prefers the world not know it possesses them. Anyway, Kennedy was quickly cut off at the pass, as the global cabal does not like to be 'outed' for their secret and diabolical actions and plans; Kennedy was assassinated by multiple operatives in a cross-fire."

"Where did you get those whacko ideas, Jameso, many people would proclaim," Ann jokingly poked at James. "Are you sure you are not from Uranus? And how does Israel fit into with the Illuminati?

"Well for sure," James mockingly replied. He had always enjoyed the quality of humor and banner between him and Ann. His remote viewing of the issue of campaign irregularities allowed him that luxury once again. "I seem to be way too close to Uranus, pardon me, but seriously, many psychics have told me I am more associated with Sirius! So Siriusly/seriously speaking, as it were, it is known that the Illuminati, especially the Rothschilds, were responsible for the creation of Israel in Palestine."

"It is the Zionist element that is part of the Illuminati Cabal, as has been revealed by numerous sources, including author Eustace Mullins, author and columnist, Michael Collins Piper and author Victor Thorn, but certainly not limited thereto. This is such an emotionally charged issue, for those of

Jewish descent, they will routinely counter with the response, "You are anti-Semitic," which is a way to label something and pejoratize and demonize it, all the while, ignoring the factual evidence supporting the reality. Even to this day, Israel steadfastly denies it has a nuclear arsenal, even as they boldly demonize the Iranians for trying to develop this weaponry."

"With President Kennedy (JFK) I believe we can state was really a friend of the American people, despite what surfaced as womanizing tendencies. After all, Marilyn Monroe never complained about such and really could not get enough of him. I admit, and embarrassingly so, because for too long I allowed my prejudice toward Catholicism to taint my view; JFK was a great president, irrespective of his 'dirty tricks' against 'Tricky Dick' Nixon."

"Wow and maybe even bow wow, ha-ha," Ann barkingly responded, "I appreciate your honesty on these subjects." Being a Catholic, at the time of JFK's election, I remember the nuns and priests exhorting us to vote for Kennedy. I was actually too young to vote, but my parents both voted for Kennedy. Thinking about our overview of past presidents and their campaign, certainly Kennedy as a Catholic president was as historic as President Obama's being elected as a black president. Now, we are on yet another precipice; a woman... Hillary Clinton being elected president."

"Undoubtedly, all these things are germane to our *summit* here," Ann, "but before we consider these things, and consider them we will, I will say this, and more soon thereafter, 'This disturbing shadow government by whatever name: Illuminati cult, conspiracy theory, is more often... actually almost always... a *conspiracy reality* and is truly the *power behind the throne.* Did you ever wonder why this topic was so thoroughly covered in the "X-Files" TV series and movies?"

"Lest I digress, we probably should jump into the Michael Dukakis—George W. Bush, presidential election campaign. It is interesting how Dukakis held a huge lead over Bush at the beginning of his presidential campaign. This may have been in part because of President Reagan's tepid endorsement of Bush, his own vice president! Do you think Reagan knew Bush—and/or the CIA Bush was a member of since 1961 (and director of in 1976-7)—was involved in his attempted assassination? Remember, Ann, when we discussed how John Hinckley was a family friend of the Bushes? And, when we are told Hinckley was a mind-controlled CIA dupe, that is certainly possible, but I ask you, does it tell us the whole story?"

"Now, getting back to Bush and Dukakis," James words flowed continuously. "We can easily ascertain that despite Reagan's lukewarm endorsement of Bush, he found a truly slimy way to cut the vote gap by taking a picture of Michael Dukakis riding around in a tank, with a helmet on his head and with a broad smile. The Bush campaign took this picture, used it in an ad, and implied Dukakis was trigger happy and too dangerous to be president! Honestly! Not to be bested, Bush found another point on which to pound Dukakis. He picked up on a prisoner furlough program Dukakis had signed as governor of Massachusetts. The program allowed a prisoner, convicted murderer, Willie Horton, to have a weekend out jail, wherein Horton raped and killed a woman. In fact, Horton was mistakenly released by the prison system but the truth was conveniently obscured. It doesn't take much to turn the tide; these two events led to Dukakis being trounced in the popular election and The Electoral College, with George W. Bush receiving more electoral votes than anyone in recent history."

"Of course you realize, Whispering James," Ann flippantly replied, "Bush got a dose of his own medicine in the next election with Bill, ('I did not have sexual relations with that woman!') Clinton. It is well known, just how easily Bill Clinton, AKA 'Slick Willie,' could charm the panties off a woman with a locked chastity belt and was a deft 'spinner' of tall tales. Early on Clinton gained a reputation as a sexual predator of many women... far beyond the publicly known Jennifer Flowers, Paula Jones, Monika Lewinsky, and Kathleen Wiley."

"On top of that, Bill's wife, Hillary Clinton, the present 2016 Democrat presidential candidate, was very active in covering up Bill's sexual dalliances, by either threatening the women to be silent about their sexual experiences and/or paying them off to do so! All of this has been most luridly chronicled in *The American Free Press* newspaper, and now further supported in Clinton adviser, Dick Morris' book, *Armageddon,* Ann revealed."

"Well, hold on to your panties," James retorted in a disgusted manner, "because what I have to share with you honestly shakes me to the core of my existence. In three books, including *Thanks for the Memories,* by Brice Taylor, *Trance-Formation of*

America, by Cathy O'Brien and Mark Phillips, and *Illuminati Defector Details Pervasive Conspiracy,* by Savali, the authors discuss in great detail child sex slavery as part of the Illuminati and you will never guess who were the presidential participants in this, Ann!"

Ann replied in a laughing manner but coupled with disgust, "Obviously, Bill Clinton, because we've long had reason to believe he is a sexual pervert and/or deviant. That is a no brainer since we know he visited "Orgy/Pedophile Island" twenty six times with billionaire, Jeffrey Epstein on his plane, outfitted with a bed so that orgy pedophile sex could be "enjoyed." Considering Bill's notorious history, it does not take a big inductive leap to realize he probably was not on this plane or island just to be a spectator.; but even if he was just observing the sexual activities, that would be almost as disgusting and repugnant. All of this was chronicled in a Fox News article."

"Well, Ann," James nodding his head up and down as he shared, "you are right on this about Bill Clinton and Hillary Clinton as well in a three way with Bill and a young girl; but there were many more president's involved. Can you believe that?

Luckily in heaven you do not have to deal with the rampant sexual perversion on Earth but when it reaches the level of our presidents, and all moral values and moral bearings become obscured. As I said, hold on to your panties, as the list of presidential perverts includes, John Kennedy, Lyndon Johnson, Ronald Reagan, George H.W. Bush, George W. Bush, There were also governors, including Lamar Alexander, Richard Thornburgh, and Bill Bennett (author of *The Book of Virtues*... Not!*); senators Patrick Leahy, Robert Byrd, Arlen Spector; and there were prime ministers, including Pierre Trudeau and Brian Mulroney. Put those turds in you pipe and smoke it, Ann!"

"Ha-ha, and nah, nah, on the smoking of turds but it might apply to these pedophilic presidents," Ann proclaimed with a disgusted amusement. "My world has been rather "rocked" by these revelations of yours! Unbelievable—almost—since these things are so distressing... really... how many people could even stand to consider this yet alone, believe it?"

"Yeah, woe is me, I need to pee, the same I can never be," James grimaced, feeling betrayed beyond all measure. It is going to be hard to continue, but let's get back to the election."

77

"Anyway, back to thinking about what George H. W. Bush was up against, Ann, I see now he had a larger problem than Slick Willie! The iconic, small of stature, yet a real 'sparkplug' of a highly successful businessman, in the form of Ross Perot, was also running for president. Almost immediately, and seemingly out of nowhere, Perot gained a huge following, much like another famous and successful businessman running for president right now, Donald J. Trump. It is interesting to look back at how the Illuminati cult had managed to get their global trade agenda into the media."

"Don't you find it equally fascinating that Ross Perot staunchly opposed the North American Free Trade Agreement (NAFTA). Bush had not only supported NAFTA but also what he termed, The New World Order (NWO), which was a subterfuge acronym for the Illuminati cult!"

"Actually, by June of 1992, the polling showed Perot had 39% of the vote, Bush 31% of the vote, and Bill Clinton at 25%," Ann continued down the path of James' chosen topic. "Even though he surged in the polls, Perot unexpectedly exited the presidential race, citing that someone in his family had been threatened because of his presidential aspirations.

Now, most people would call this a 'conspiracy theory' yet we have at least two examples: JFK and Ronald Reagan, each of which indicates people who threaten the agenda of the Illuminati —and if you do not like that articulation—persons or groups with dubious agendas, have historically eliminated the forces of opposition or at least attempt to do as in Reagan's case. With Perot now out of the race, Clinton's poll rating soared to 58% and Bush remained at 31%. Well, in the beginning of October, Perot jumped back into the race but never again approached anything like his previous polling numbers of 39%, languishing at around 8%."

"So," Ann continued intently, "we should raise the question of whether George H.W. Bush or Bill Clinton were behind the threats to Ross Perot, since they both have been tied to people who were attacked and/or killed. Once again, this is akin to one of those duhlicious moments where the fruit is not really delicious."

"Well, for me, *mon amour*, " James cooed, "you are bringing us back to a pivotal time in the U.S. Although I fervently believe, yet cannot prove, Perot could have won the election and been instrumental in changing the destructive effects of free trade on the populace at large, in the form of vanishing jobs, and U.S. industries. Now, would Perot have been assassinated if he won the election? From what you and I know, Ann, that is almost impossible to discount!"

"So, lets look at Bill Clinton, Ann, who said he would never support NAFTA, even as George H. W. Bush did. Well, he did win the election, but only to ram NAFTA through the senate, as an agreement— although it was a treaty requiring a 2/3 approval in the Senate. Meanwhile, our Nation is left with the legacy of the Clinton's. The only good thing we can say about their two-term presidency is at least Bill kept us from being sucked into the Serbian-Croatian-Bosnian War, unlike the entanglements we experienced under President George W. Bush. He also purportedly balanced the federal budget but with rather disastrous consequences to the long term financial health of the United States."

"I know this is a delicate subject, Ann, but there is some contention Bill's sexcapades with Monica Lewinsky may not have been limited only to him but to Hillary, as well. You know *The American Free Press* newspaper uncovered evidence of Hillary having lesbian affairs and when you put two and two together, and think of how often you've heard the phrases, maybe what Bill Clinton meant when he said, 'I did not have sexual relations with that woman,' he was referring to Hillary rather than Monica, ha!"

"Laughing my ass off, and ha-ha, flaw, flaw, you are really a hoot with some toot, oh James of the trumpet playing lips," Ann comically replied. "Bill Clinton boasted that he had balanced the federal budget, an admirable achievement, for sure, until you realize how this was done, which was by raiding Social Security Trust Fund reserves and selling off U.S. gold bullion from Fort Knox."

"Republican Ron Paul, and former Libertarian presidential candidate, introduced bills in congress to audit the Federal Reserve and the contents of Fort Knox, Kentucky, where U.S. gold bullion is supposed to be stored. Now this is where things took on the color of devious and fascinating, some time ago, when U.S. stamped gold bullion wound up in China. When bars of bullion were weighed, they came up a few grams short of the weight they should have had. Can you imagine! The bars were cut in half and lo and behold, they were revealed to not be pure gold at all, but rather tungsten gold-plated bars. Now tell me, totally aside from the Chinese government being fleeced, aren't Americans obliged to consider at least two things: First, is there even any gold bullion left in Fort Knox and secondly, if there is gold in Ft. Knox, is it only tungsten gold-plated bars?"

"Wow and pow and Kung pau chicken, to wit," James was shaking his head back and forth, in amazement while laughing derisively. "I know you know I am laughing, Ann, and probably what I am going to share about there being no gold bullion in the New York Federal Reserve Bank. There have been reports from confidential sources that the N.Y. Fed gold has been sold several times over, in the form of derivatives."

"Irrespective of this, we can fairly surmise there is a great shortage of gold bullion in the N.Y. Fed. Indonesia asked to have their gold, which was being stored there, returned to Indonesia. The Fed agreed, but later reneged on the agreement, after sending only a small amount of bullion to Indonesia. The same thing happened when Germany asked for their stored gold to be returned. An agreement was reached, a little bullion was returned and then again, the Fed reneged on its agreement! These parasite bankers, part of the private Federal Reserve System, can be directly traced back to the Rothschilds, Warburgs, The Vatican Bank and the Zionist banking interests, all under the umbrella of the Illuminati cult. Take those beans and crunch them, Ann!"

"Hey, James," Ann cheerily proclaimed, "you can take those beans, refry them and then plate them in gold, ha!. It is interesting, even in our digression, most of these circles back to presidential politics. So now that we are back, why don't we look at one of the closest presidential elections of all time, between George W. Bush and Ozone Al Gore, vice president under Bill Clinton. Both candidates had extensive opposition research operations, trying to dig as much dirt up about each other as possible."

"Gore made things easy for Bush by claiming he invented the Internet and grew up on a farm in Tennessee, neither of which was true. It was true Gore's father, who was a career politician himself, Al Gore Sr., did own a large tobacco plantation. Gore was a self-proclaimed champion of environmental issues, including *global warming*, but Bush research showed the decisions Gore and Clinton made were anything but environmentally friendly, allowing many businesses to be gross polluters. What we cannot forget is the manner in which pollution went through the roof in Mexico after NAFTA was passed; it allowed many American companies to relocate and manufacture without any pollution controls."

"Bush, on the other hand," continued Ann," was found to have many drunk driving convictions and also evaded the Vietnam War by joining the Air National Guard; he even failed to legally fulfill that commitment. What the Gore campaign never seized upon was the regular drug trafficking of cocaine into the Mena Airport in Arkansas by George W. and Jeb Bush. This might have been because Bill Clinton, the governor of Arkansas, provided cover for this CIA operation. Many reporters in *The American Free Press* newspaper, whose reputation for accuracy is legendary, covered all these little-known issues in many articles."

"There were also accurate accusations that Bush was into "sex, drugs, and rock and roll" and highly addicted to sexual escapades. What really damaged Gore's candidacy, however, was Ralph Nader's entry into this presidential contest, as a defender of the consumer and protector of the environment, which effectively siphoned votes away from Gore but not Bush."

"I am well aware of this and despite all the perceived charges and the countercharges," James smugly proclaimed, "it was the computerized voting used in this presidential election that led to some highly skewed results. The exit polls taken in Pennsylvania, Ohio and Florida revealed Al Gore won those states, although the poll tallies indicated otherwise. So if Gore had one any one of these three states, he would have won the election and from what I have seen, it appears he won all three."

"So, Ann, as *The American Free Press* newspaper covered in great depth, there were actually employees from the computerized voting program company, owned by billionaire George Soros who were discovered going into the computer room without a poll worker, as required by law. It does not take too much of an inductive leap to conclude something was done to the voting program to alter the results in Florida, Pennsylvania, and Ohio; and, by the way, this same George Soros is part of the Illuminati cult, who we know will always put their interests before the populace... us!"

As James continued sharing all he had learned, he elaborated to Ann, "In Florida we had another computerized voting system that punched out small pieces of paper. There were so many problems with this system the Florida Supreme Court ordered a manual recount of the votes, because of a suit filed by Al Gore. Florida governor, Jeb Bush, who just coincidentally was the brother of presidential candidate, George W. Bush, ordered state election officials to cease their recount, and subsequent foiled the recount."

"I knew someone whose father actually worked on the creation of this *chad paper* system and he revealed to me the ballots were so delicate it was impossible to manually recount them accurately, as chads of paper would break lose from the candidates names when they were handled by hand, and made for multiple indications on candidates for a specific office. Anyway, George W. Bush became president of the United States; part of his claim to fame being only the second father-son president combos in U.S. history, with his father, George H.W. Bush; the first combo being President John Adams and his son, John Quincy Adams."

"How fascinating and revealing all this is," Ann was intent as she responded, "since some people have said this is the day 'democracy died', when the election results were modified in favor of George W. Bush. Yet from what you and I have garnered, James, it appears democracy started dying more than two hundred years ago. When you and I used to talk to people about this many decades ago, their eyes would either glaze over into a stupor or they would heatedly disagree with us. Oh well! Oh hell, welcome to Dr. Newton's book, *Planet of the Stupids: Bringing the Light of God to Planet Earth—With a Paradise Found.*"

"*Mama mia y Papa tio*, I know you love that book, James, as do I, since you did the research for the book for Dr. Newton," Ann pointedly reminded him. "I know, as a Scorpio, that deceit and lies and intrigue really bug the crap out of you! I'm just wondering, do you have the stomach to look at two, James?"

"Yes, Ann, you may just have to hit me in the head with a cast iron pan to mitigate the accompanying pain and disappointment," James sardonically replied. But first, let us look at the dynamic events that transpired under the two-term president, George W. Bush, who I often refer to as 'George the Junior.' As well as him being younger he would also seem intellectually inferior to his father, or any other president."

"Yes, he is cunning and charming but that does not necessarily translate into intelligence, wisdom or compassion. Now, From what I have been able to gather from many sources, the attack on the Trade Towers, on Sept. 11, 2001, was not engineered by President Bush, but it is hard to fathom he didn't really know what was about to happen, considering all the intelligence and data gathering by the FBI, CIA and NSA!"

"So I know from this statement many people going to roll their eyes and pejoratively consider it a 'conspiracy theory.' However, from hacked emails, there has been evidence of heavy involvement in the destruction of this building by the Saudi Royal Family, supposedly a U.S. ally, through the funding and operatives, such as the Bin Laden family. If these sources are correct, the despised Osama Bin Laden was a part of the Saudi Royal Family, involved in the assault on the Trade Towers."

"We can also know from certain events as the Trade Towers were collapsing, that Jewish elites and businessmen, including Larry Silverstein, who held the master lease on the Trade Towers complex, were gleeful, from a distance, as they were filmed in both New York and New Jersey, in a party-like atmosphere. It would seem someone had to tell NORAD, our plane defense force, to stand down that fateful day. And we also have to factor in the two Israeli companies that make the software, Ptech and MITRE, both of which are capable of paralyzing air defenses. Is this where we put two and two together?"

"Hey James. The Whale Whisperer, are you sure you want to go into this, since you are recording our dialogue and there will be many people who will call you anti-Semitic just for what you have said so far?" Ann's query was deeply colored with tones of concern for James.

"Well, I appreciate your concern, Angelic One, but I will just chop people off at the knees who bring this up and this is how!" James responded. I honor the Jewish traditions and in specific, The *72 Names of God from* Exodus 14, versus 19-21, and I also know how to recite and read them in Hebrew.

89

Everything these names stand for, such as the 7th Name of God, Aleph Kaf Aleph, which means to restore things to their perfect state, is antithetical to everything promulgated by the Zionists that have a firm control of the nation of Israel. I would be astonished if even one Zionist would even know of or incorporate these names into their daily lives. I would wager they are much too busy studying the Talmud, which considers Gentiles as Goyum (cattle to be herded and slaughtered)."

"Wow! Your *chutzpah* is starkly evident here James," Ann stated in amazement. "I remember way back when we were at an Israel War Bond event and you asked me even in the 1970's, why Americans and American Jews were necessary to fund the state of Israel, which is already a thriving country. They talked about poor, defenseless Israel all evening long."

"Certain and most true," James stated as he shared his growing exasperation with Ann. "George the Junior generally surrounded himself with the worst people possible... maybe they were picked by his father and/or Illuminati operatives. First, he had Dick Cheney as his vice-president, a man we know to be deeply involved in the CIA, the Black Water

Group (now The Kraft Group) of mercenaries, which means soldiers and assassins for hire. Then you had Paul Wolfowitz, Douglas Feith, Michael Chertoff and Richard Perle in heading U.S. defense departments and Intelligence groups. All of these men are either Israeli—U.S. dual citizens and/or have ties to the Israeli Mossad."

"So why should all this be of any importance, James?" Ann asked, in a somewhat investigative tone.

"Ha-ha, I was hoping you would step into that trap and ask me such," James mockingly replied. "So I will share my thoughts here! There were over on hundred Mossad agents arrested in the U.S. They were here on visas posing as art students but were actually here expressly to penetrate our defense and intelligence operations, just before 9-11. One or two operatives we could consider as random but, over a hundred shows a campaign of espionage."

"Why were they not indicted or prosecuted? There were Mossad agents gathered around the 911 crime scene who were arrested as well, yet nary a one was indicted or prosecuted? Why, Ann? It is impossible for me to believe something of this nature this could happen unless there were orders passed down from high level Bush administration officials... almost all who were Jewish dual citizens, Zionist, and/or Mossad, but more importantly, who were known to have divided loyalties. Although there is no direct evidence of who used the Ptech and MITRE computer programs that disabled our air defenses and NORAD, just from observation, it is safe to assume Bush and Cheney and their Zionist/Mossad cabinet members and department heads let Israel take control of the United States, if not *de jure*, then certainly *de facto*."

"Is that Israel being a friend to America, Ann? Looking at myriad Christians goose-stepping to the tunes and propaganda coming out of Israel; I wonder, have they been bamboozled into believing the lies about how Israel loves Christians? Just look around, the reality remains, Christians are treated better in Iran than Israel and the New Testament is routinely burned in Israel. Hard to believe how gullible people are but...! You know, Ann, when I get wrapped in this ugly mire, I keep coming back to Jesus' words in the book of John, '...by their works ye shall know them.'"

"Well, James, I am impressed! You have certainly cast a new light on things rarely, if every illumined, but I wanted to ask you about Larry Silverstein, the Jewish business man who bought the master lease to the Trade Tower complex. Even to me it seems odd that would have occurred just seven short weeks before the towers collapsed!"

"What a topic! I can't believe how ripe and rife with unbelievable information." Ann attempted to squelch her sarcasm as she further commented, "Certainly I could share many things about that but will concentrate on just one or two things. Right after Silverstein's purchase, entire floors of Towers One, Two and Seven were shut down, supposedly for routine maintenance, as was reported in several articles in *The American Free Press* newspaper. What were they doing? Could they have been placing thermite demolition explosives on the inner steel columns in the elevator shaft?"

"I ask these questions for two reasons: First, it is impossible for anyone to refute the pools of thermite demolition explosive, which were found in the pit of the collapsed buildings. And second, the manner in which the two towers collapsed is exactly like what happens in a thermite charged controlled

93

demolition; each level pancakes on the level of the building below it. Additionally, both policemen and firemen inside of the building have reported hearing successive boom, boom, boom, etc., exactly what happens in a controlled demolition. Even if, as we were led to believe jet fuel could cut through structural steel—which it absolutely cannot—the upper part of the building would have fallen to the side, leaving the level of the building intact. My God! If we put everything together, especially knowing that jet fuel, which burns at 1600° F could not melt structural steel beams that melt at 2300° F, we can recognize we have been told fairy tales about this event. Terrorist Unicorns keep coming to mind and what a ruse they are!"

"And can you believe this, Ann? In the Utah State engineering department Professor Smith had pointed out the very facts you shared and then was promptly fired from his professorship. One can certainly assume he not only hit on some important facts, but disturbed someone's raw nerves, as well. Bush's Mossad/Zionist posse knew they could not allow Smith's work to be made available to or considered by the citizens of our country." And also remember, Ann, when I told you previously about a U.S. bomber that crashed into the Empire State

Building during World War II, which not so surprisingly sustained no structural collapse."

"I do remember you talking about that James, the Demolition Whisperer, and also how it would be impossible for Muslim terrorists trained on Piper Cub airplanes to have flown and piloted commercial jet planes into the Trade Towers. Each of these facts certainly confirms your statements!"

Gloating, James proclaimed, "But here is the smoking gun of all smoking guns, Ann. How is it that Tower Seven of the complex collapsed and nary a plane was flown into it?" On top of that, Ann, there is a recording that supports the fact that the BBC actually reported the collapse of Tower Seven several minutes before it occurred! Even if people think everything previous to this is like looneysville, and I am looney as well, the people who ignore what happened at Tower Seven are most likely ensconced in the rare ethers of 'Never, Never Land' and flying around therein with Tinker Belle and Peter Pan, ha-ha. We might also ask, 'Was a plane supposed to have been crashed into Tower Seven?'"

"You know me, Ann; I don't have any intention to be mean here... just wake up the populace to the fact what they have been told about 911 should be relegated to the land of myths and fairytales. There are those who would produce movies about the event, but rest assured, many of them would not contain the remotest vestiges of truth, although there are some documentaries such as *Fahrenheit 9 11* and *In Plane Sight* that are both revealing and illuminating."

"I know it pains you, James, just how very gullible people are about trusting their government. Am I right, oh Demolition Whisperer?" Ann asked. She was always sensitive to James' feelings, and hoped he understood how deep was her empathy now about his consternation for the state of his country.

"If I was Bush the Junior I would never again show my face in public, with the tainted legacy he has," James proclaimed. "I am sure the dual citizen Jewish/Mossad/Zionist sympathizers, advisers and department heads, such as Richard Perle, Paul Wolfowitz, etc. were the ones urging him to invade Afghanistan, as well as Dick Cheney, so Osama Bin Laden could be captured and killed."

"We could just go on and on with this conversation, Ann. In fact, I could add so much more about this country but let's cut it short; suffice it to say after spending several trillion dollars on the war there, the country is more destabilized than before we entered the fray... oh, and what about the massive opium poppy fields all over the country! Now who could those opium poppies possibly belong to, Ann? Could it be the CIA as has often been claimed... funds for 'black operations' not part of the government budgetary process?"

"Well, well—well, well," Ann exclaimed, "you have me thinking the same would apply to Iraq where the same nefarious group of dual citizens and traitors made up all the lies about Saddam Hussein having weapons of mass destruction." Ann continued, "After the expenditure of many trillions of dollars, the only 'mass destruction' I see in Iraq is that we destabilized a country. The Iraqi's were so fortunate to have us liberate them in a perpetual state of hell, where there are bombing and killings every day. Nice work, not, I must say!"

"So true, what you say, oh, Angelic Ann, " James replied. "This all circles back to the Civil War where the bankers funding both sides of a conflict, so they win regardless of which side prevails in the conflict. The privately owned Federal Reserve System is included in these parasitical bankers who steal away the vitality of an economy using exorbitant interest rates charged on money created of thin air. This banking Ponzi scheme makes Bernie Madoff look like small potatoes. Madoff created a smaller Ponzi scheme he ran within the larger Ponzi scheme of the Federal Reserve Bank. Anyway, I have had more than enough of the stench of Bush the Junior, so let's move to another president!"

"With that said, Demolition Whisperer, we can move to the current president, Barak Obama," Ann exclaimed, as she tried to move things along. "So for sure, Donald Trump has given himself grief for bringing up the citizenship status of Barak Obama, which was really sparked again by Hillary Clinton in the 2008 Democratic primary. We should mention, even emphasize, there are some sources who feel there were voting irregularities in the 2008 primary and even in the general election with John McCain, but I know you have a lot of specifics regarding the citizenship status of Obama, right, James?"

"Yes, Ann, your question could be answered in the affirmative. First, Barak Obama's grandparents in Kenya have consistently bragged about him being born in Kenya, so that would disqualify him from U.S. citizenship unless he was naturalized," James acerbically stated. Secondly, if you do more than quickly glance at the Hawaiian birth certificates provided by Obama, you would pick up on the fact they do not have numbers that would correspond with his age. Thirdly, some document experts have concluded the birth certificate has been forged. Fourth, at all the schools Obama claimed to attend, no one seems to have a recollection of him being in attendance at any of them, including Occidental College or Harvard. I wonder then, Ann, does that not leave us with an illegal alien president who has stated ever so boldly, 'The Constitution is outdated and an obstacle to progress?' This is what pains me: the legacy of this presidency will be extremely high unemployment and under employment at a rate of 25%, eight million more people on food stamps than when he took office, declining wages for almost all workers except very high level corporate executive and managers, an increasing crime and murder rate and amplified terrorism worldwide. Obama seems determined to push through the Trans-Pacific

Partnership (TPP) that is beneficial to corporate interests, but in no way shape or form, beneficial for the populace… the masses struggling to survive in an anemic economy that pays wages too low to live on! Obama also seems concerned with "global integration" and the elimination of country borders and country sovereignty, as demonstrated in his recent comments to the U.N."

I guess that brings us to the faux solution to healthcare: *The Affordable (Not!) Healthcare Act* (Obamacare; *if only he did care about us*]), promoted as a panacea, yet being anything but such," James continued. Ann noticed he was directly and highly agitated by the president's lies as he continued, "The deceptive illegal alien president forgot to tell people who already had insurance coverage their premiums would increase from 50% to 150%. That is nothing remotely close to affordable and has no vestiges of care and caring, ha!"

"Most of our nation's physicians do not want to take Obamacare patients because they are paid too little to care of them, and insurance companies are pulling out of the insurance pool that underwrites The Affordable Care Act because they are losing money on the Obamacare policies, which will raise prices more, and competition among companies will dwindle."

"To compound things, when the Obamacare nightmare was litigated before the U.S. Supreme Court, the court ruled in favor of retaining this healthcare nightmare by relying on *The Interstate Commerce Act*, which has been used to justify all kinds of illegal babble. How on earth can people miss the fact there is no inherent tie to interstate commerce and personal health? How can we accept the Supreme Court concocting an inane faux logic to support such? Forcing people to buy healthcare, as Obamacare does, is a violation of individual liberty... unless it is a part of a socialism... actually totalitarian Communism; and that takes us back to Dr. Newton's, *Planet of the Stupids: Bringing the Light of God to Planet Earth—With a Paradise Found,* George Orwell's, *Animal Farm,* and Aldous Huxley's *1984* and *Brave New World.*

"For myself, Ann, and hopefully for you," James exclaimed, tasting the sarcasm in his voice, "I don't need or want a president full of pooh telling me what to do, how I should think, or whether I should wink; and I certainly do not need him telling me about the dangers of global warming, when we are

close to entering an Ice Age, something we covered previously re Ozone Al Gore/Bore. This president also has gone out of his way to encourage Illegal alien voters, to use the names of dead registered voters and this is probably what allowed him to get elected in both the first and second elections. Please don't worry about truth and fairness... just shiite on them! This was well documented in a study by Old Dominion University."

"Then we have this illegal alien president who has de facto assumed the role of emperor, signing things into law through the process of Executive Order," James continued his passionate indictment. "Yet we have to hold Congress as complicit in this because they will not revoke the *War Powers Act* of either Abraham Lincoln or Franklin D. Roosevelt. So this man, masquerading as our president but acting like an emperor, circumvents the legislative process to promote his personal agenda."

"Remember, he clearly stated, 'The Constitution is outdated and an obstacle to progress.' However, maybe the worst of Obama's crimes is just making things up about people and events that do not have even one finger in the 'pool of reality.' When I think about it, Ann, I am sure Hitler is looking down in envy at just how slick this president is through his mastery of every propaganda trick in the book! Of course this would apply to Bill and Hillary Clinton, as well!"

CHAPTER IV

A TRAIL OF DECEIT WHERE TRUTH WE NEVER MEET!

———∞∞———

THE EXASPERATED, ANGELIC Ann declared, "Good God, Whale Whisperer, you have not come up for air for about five or six minutes! You are sucking up the entire atmosphere, James, ha-ha. So let's move to Obama's designated successor, Hillary Clinton, the presidential candidate who rigged the Democratic primaries, against her challenger, the popular Bernie Sanders, who most likely should be the Democratic candidate."

"This brings up an interesting observation as well, and that is how much more likeable and electable Bernie Sanders is than Hillary Clinton, and every poll indicated such, but let's jump back into the 2008 election, when I was sure Hillary Clinton would receive the Democratic Party nomination, as were you, and out of nowhere comes Senator Barak Obama. For a while, Hillary led the race and then somehow, someway, the relatively unknown Obama started gaining momentum and barely garnered the nomination.

As Ann continued, cherishing her chance to get in a few words edgewise, "Now people are still scratching their heads today over what happened to Clinton. I had the same queries running rampant in my mind until the hacked Democratic National Convention emails were shared into the public realm and we have direct admissions between Debbie Wasserman Schultz, Democratic National Chairperson and Hillary Clinton—talking about how Bernie Sanders could not be allowed to win the 2016 Democratic Party nomination. So right away, my mind drifts back to the election of 2000 and how the exit polls showed Ozone Al Gore won the election by popular vote, yet he did not become president. The final outcome of this election was one of the closest in the nation's history, so could we at the very worst, speculate computerized voting tallies are being manipulated, or there was voter fraud where illegal aliens were voting, as supported by the study at Old Dominion University... or both?

James was extremely focused as he made his next comment to Ann, "So let's get into some proof of this, shall we? Mathematician, Richard Charmin, with two Masters' Degrees in applied mathematics, says, '...there are strong indications of voting irregularities in the Democratic primaries in 2008 and 2016.' The great disparity between the exit polls in the 2016 New York Democratic primary and the actual vote tallies would tip us off to such. I will come back to this a little later, Ann, but we are certainly turning over some rather *disturbing stones,* which reveal an outright plot to disenfranchise the American voter by the major political parties, duh!"

"The Republican National Committee was trying to do the same to Trump, by engaging all sources to prevent him acquiring the nomination, through a set of arbitrary and biased party primary rules. Which leads us to an important 2016 study by Stanford University, which reports there are definite indications of voting irregularities in the current 2016 Democratic primaries. Now, this Stanford study goes on to quantify that states with lax voting laws are those where there has been significant voting fraud therein. More and more, people inside the Democratic Party are waking up to this fraud in their primaries, yet there seems little concern when it happens in general elections."

"Do you suppose this is why I'm often inclined to call Democrats, Dumbacrats, yet equally, could the Republicans not be called Republicons? The political parties simply do not—and maybe never did or will—care about the majority of people want, and we saw that looking back into those old elections, too, Ann!"

"Hey James," Ann pointedly exclaimed, don't you find it astonishing when the Democratic National Committee ((DNC) and Hillary Clinton railed out at the Russians, for purportedly hacking the emails, that showed they were skewing the primary results and even blaming Donald Trump for encouraging the Russians to do such, rather than apologizing for their cheating and deceitful behavior? They ignored the real issue, as though nothing had happened and instead talked about how bad the Russians were, and President Vladimir Putin, in particular. The DNC actions show a blatant disregard for the democratic process and inculcate crime and fraud of Chicago style machine politics, which is really the *school* where Communist, Saul Alinsky, trained Obama."

"I am hoping, Ann, that readers will take time to validate what I say is true; there is not much available in mainstream press but there is in the alternative press, such as *The American Free Press Newspaper* and Judicial Watch and I am surprised at how few people are aware of information validating Obama being a Communist's disciple!"

"While Alinsky and his frightening Communist miasmic nightmare agenda is most odious and malodorous," James exclaimed as he held his nose; "there is a most disagreeable stench that follows Hillary Clinton, wherever she goes. Yes, supposedly she worked on a project in the late 1980's that benefitted children and that is a good thing. Since then, the 'good' has grown rather non-existent, starting with the fraudulent Whitewater land deal, which was part of the Rose Law Firm, with James McDougall, senior partner, for whom Hillary worked and was deeply involved."

"The primary problem with Whitewater was how the development project went 'belly up' and the investors therein walked away with nothing in the bankruptcy, basically because the duo of McDougall and Clinton had already skimmed off millions of dollars into their bank accounts. Wait a minute! Don't you remember, Ann, when the Clinton's, Hillary and Billary, decried how poor they were when they left the White House. They are quite the jokesters, don't you think, Ann?"

"Jokesters they most definitely be, but the real joke is on we," Ann laughingly replied to James. "Even if that were true, and almost all sources consider their poverty status to be complete B.S., with the so called Clinton Charitable Trust, any vestiges of poverty were wiped from the Clinton's. When Hillary was secretary of state, under Obama, she routinely used her power to extract tributes and bribes so gain contributions to their trust in return U.S. government access and favors. This ran the gamut of accepting 'contributions' from Middle Eastern nations with draconian laws and attitudes toward women! It also involved Hillary facilitating a Russian state owned company, Rozatom, acquiring control over twenty percent of the U.S. uranium supply."

"The *sellout* of the Willow Creek Mine in the uranium rich state of Wyoming is well documented, as are Russia's refusal to abide by the mining laws to protect people in that area from chemical spills, etc. So this egregious act, is not only illegal within the parameters of the job of secretary of state, it definitely compromises national security. But again, things like violating national security, certainly have never stopped Hillary and Billary (Bill Clinton) from doing whatever they wanted."

"Billary was also paid exorbitant speaking fees for countries who curried favor with Hillary, and funneled into the charitable trust. The Clinton Charitable trust only donates ten percent of its income to charity so we might ask where the rest is going and the obvious answer is into the hands of the Clinton family, sans a standard of trust, as it were! Also, the Clinton Charitable Trust was in charge of the Haitian earthquake relief effort and very little of that aid made it to the Haitian people and much equipment sent for relief seemed to vanish into thin air (code for the equipment being stolen)."

"One of the many sources regarding the misdealing of the Clinton's charitable funds for Haiti is documented by Dinesh D'Souza in a new film and book, both entitled: *Hillary's America: The Secret History of the Democratic Party.*"

"Well, regarding that faux charitable trust, more akin to a slush fund, again, of which only, at the most 10% is donated to charity. There is also word on the street it also launders money through a Canadian bank and the last time I checked, Ann—correct me if I am wrong—money laundering is felony, a violation of RICO laws," James shouted with gusto!

"Since you are the attorney, James, I don't know why you are asking me about this, but of course you are correct," Ann responded.

"Well, of course, you are my judge and jury," explained James, "so I am glad you have delivered your verdict, ha-ha!"

"Nothing suspends how many people have come to believe the Clinton Charitable Trust is really nothing more than the Clinton's personal piggy bank, and we as citizens, and most certainly Donald Trump should be pounding on this issue," returned Ann. "Hilary is criticizing Trump for having close ties with Russia and its president, Vladimir Putin, and somehow this makes him dangerous and unfit to be president, which might be a valid syllogism but based on false premises, so disingenuous at its core! You know, if I were Trump, I would reveal how Hillary's facilitating the sale of uranium to Russia damages our national security!"

"You are so right! That national security issue should be wrapped tightly around Hillary's neck, ha-ha," James sardonically declared. "The fact that she actively engineered the overthrow of President Mommar Kaddafi, throwing Libya into chaos, and making it a terrorist paradise, disproves she is even remotely concerned about national security and more about destabilizing things."

"Then it appears the nerve gas held in Libya was sent to ISIS. Now I know this ISIS attribution will raise more than some eyebrows... maybe pony tails too, and yet I have seen enough evidence that convinces me this is a valid statement. ISIS has been decoded as Israeli Secret Intelligence Service, so there seems to be an Israeli connection to the chaos in the Middle East through a funding of ISIS, and other evidence points to funding also from the U.S. and NATO... let us be under no illusions here, a real dangerous situation has been deliberately created. The Libyan nerve gas that was used in Syria was blamed on President Bashar Assad, yet where the gassing took place Assad had already stationed troops so... tell me, why he would gas his own troops that are already undermanned in the civil war in Syria! It seems more likely ISIS and not Syrian military forces used the nerve gas."

"Wow, in how," Ann proclaimed. "Your analysis is brutal but right on point. Vladimir Putin has been beaten up, by incessant propaganda on Russia's intervention in Syria and his bombing of ISIS forces, the same forces being funded by the West and Israel, which leads to destabilized countries. So if Russia is destroying ISIS forces, as it is, this leads to a much safer world. As you said, James, let us be under no illusions... we can clearly see Hillary Clinton, and her boss, Barak Obama, created an unsafe world and deliberately so... but **why?**"

"Now, in how, "James remarked in response to Ann's assessment of things. "This could naturally lead us to Hillary Clinton's using mutual private servers (mostly cell phones) to conduct state business when she was secretary of state. Hillary has committed perjury many times by actively lying about myriad issues, claiming for the most part the communication on private servers, as opposed to a secure government server. Such gall should taste bitter in Hillary's mouth; despite her assurances to the contrary, it has been proven on numerous occasions she received classified documents on her personal servers. These servers that were ultimately also hacked. This was even substantiated by FBI director, James Comey, who is known to have mentioned 33,000 missing or destroyed emails, after they were subpoenaed by the U.S. Congress." In the last days of the debate, an increasing number of questionable emails surfaced, making the public aware of her history of less than credible practices.

"So what should we say about the woman who has had the audacity to call Donald Trump not presidential and dangerous... the woman who has actually exhibited and established pejorative assertions by her own perjuries and the actions related thereto? 'Lying Hillary,' as 'The Donald' proclaims?"

"Well, we know these issues are substantiated by many sources, such as *The American Free Press* newspaper, *Judicial Watch*, the Pew Organization, and the emails leaked by Julian Assange's,' Wiki Leaks.'

"Well, you are not too far... from the truth that is," as words flowed freely from Ann's lips, "There is an issue many consider too hot to discuss or consider and that is the trail of dead bodies, in the wake of the Clinton's, many of them listed as suicides and yet the ballistic and forensic evidence, disproves the suicide theories."

"The most notable example of this is the purported suicide of Vince Foster, white house aid and Hillary's boyfriend. So there was a business deal gone sour in which both Foster and Hillary were involved. Hillary told Foster he should take the 'fall' alone and he told her, 'no way,' as revealed by confidential source, shared in *The American Free Press* newspaper. Soon after their tiff, Vince Foster wound up dead in his own car in Washington, D.C. Why do you suppose the park police ruled it a suicide, when independent ballistics and forensic experts subsequently reported the angle the bullet went through Foster's head made suicide with the weapon found, as impossible? Other notable witnesses that could have testified against Hillary in legal proceedings, namely Ron Brown, Commerce Secretary in the Bill Clinton presidential cabinet, wound up dying in a plane flown into the side of a mountain. There are at least fifty-two other mysterious and suspicious deaths in the wake of the Clinton's. Trump might be wise to bring these things up and then again, he might wind of mysteriously dead if he did, so..."

"How now, brown cow, Bill Clinton is a sexual predator, bow wow," poetically responded James. "Bill Cosby is a sexual predator to wit, yet only he is being hit! So the 'hit' means he has been indicted. The difference between the two B.C.'s is Bill Clinton has a wife who covers and protects him from the women who come forward to reveal their unwanted encounters with Bill."

"It bears worth repeating, the book written by Clinton political aide Dick Morris, *Armageddon*, reveals, Hillary actively threatened Bill Clinton's victims with harm or they were paid off to end their accusations. Secret Service Agent, Gary Byrne, was part of the Secret Service detail in the Clinton Whitehouse and verifies Dick Morris' claims in his book, *Crisis of Confidence*. If only Bill Cosby had a wife that defended him like Hillary, he might not even be facing the current charges for rape! Oh well, oh hell, the well of deceit is not nice and neat, but very, very deep!"

"Now to *The Trump*, who the Republicans have tried to dump but in their amazement, were not able to stump... or even stop, for that matter," James continued as he was on a roll. "So no Republican emails have surfaced showing a deliberate effort to stop the outsider Republican, Trump, who is cast in a similar mold to Ronald Reagan, yet their actions speak louder than any words. Reagan riled the Republican establishment by his 'outsider' ideas, in the same manner, as has done Trump. There are such arbitrary and undemocratic nuances in the Republican primaries rules of 2016 so that one might only conclude there is a deliberate effort by the party to pick its nominee, in contravention to will of the capable people of our nation selecting such."

"Evidence of these undemocratic tendencies of the Republican National Committee is reflected in the establishment Republicans found in the actions of Gov. Mitt Romney, Sen. John McCain, and the

Bush family. Not only do they not support the Republican nominee, Donald Trump, but excoriate him as unfit for the presidency. Apparently they are blind or unaware of how unqualified Clinton is as a money launder, rampant perjurer, and one who comprises national security by allowing the sale of military materials. Additionally, just who are these people to stand in judgment? Those listed above did little more than fail as presidential candidates or served pathetically as presidents, as best!"

James continued in his Whale Whisperer mode, "There is no doubt, Donald Trump is a brash and uncouth person at times, and has even been called misogynistic by his Democratic Party detractors. As to the misogynistic accusations, there is probably no other company in America that can boast almost half their executives are women... and women who are paid equivalent to men, in all employment levels."

"So this evidence strongly contraindicates misogyny exhibited by Trump or his organization. However, constructive misogyny is rife both in the Clinton Charitable Trust and in Hillary Clinton's senate staff, where women in equivalent jobs to men are paid only seventy percent for the same jobs. Hillary pounds home the propaganda that Trump is mean to women yet Hillary's wage scale for women might be considerably meaner. Just the double talk babble this woman can summon would stun even someone mentally challenged, duh!"

"Are you coming up for air… are you coming up for air… are you coming up for air, Whale Whisperer, Ann impatiently exclaimed.

"Are you talking to me… are you talking to me… or are you talking to the Whale Whisperer," James laughingly questioned Ann.

"Yes," Ann shared her words with James, "I am talking to James, the Whale Whisperer and any other *nom/*name that can be conjured up referring to *The James.*"

"Ok, then, the Whale Whisperer from the state of California defers to the most Angelic Ann from Heaven, and gives her the floor… or at least the use thereof, because he does not own the floor, ha-ha!"

"Groovy, then," Ann declared. "I am leaving 'mime mode' and the breathless state of Samadhi *(a yogic breathing protocol that can lead to suspension of breathing for periods at a time*) and will speak about other matters related to all of this."

"I really wanted to point out how Trump made a contribution to a charity of the Florida Attorney General—to make an investigation of fraud in the Trump University go away? We also find Trump really does not donate much money to his own charitable trust but at least does not use it as a piggy bank, as do Hillary and Billary. Additionally, although Trump could legally declare bankruptcy on some Atlantic City casinos, there are certainly aspects of moral reprehensiveness... after all, what contractor deserves to be cheated out of their money, unless be it for substandard and/or incomplete work? And James, you know that only too well, since you have been involved in landscape and construction projects where that happened to you, and a very bad taste it left in your mouth, isn't that true James?"

"James and the 'Whale Whisperer' answer in the affirmative... that nasty taste of not being paid for your work never goes away," James shared with Ann. "We should also bring up the charges that Trump called the Miss Universe winner in 1996, Alicia Machado, 'Miss Piggy,' when she gained weight after winning the contest. Of course such terms are offensive and yet the rules of the beauty pageant were that the winner must remain fit and beautiful. So Machado claimed Trump bullied her and this caused her eating and psychological disorders. Yet she previously mentioned she had eating disorders before the Miss Universe contest and eating disorders are always associated with psychological problems."

"What a nasty can of worms we have opened here, James," Ann sarcastically volunteered. "So as I was a woman on Earth, I really do not like being judged on my body image and yet in the context of this hullabaloo, and what the Miss Universe contestants agree to, Alicia Machado was guilty of breach of contract. It seems as though the Clinton 'dirt mining machine' has worked overtime to marginalize Donald Trump."

"Also," Ann hurriedly continued, so as to get a few words edgewise in before James, the Whale Whisperer, "we have another issue where Trump used crude language to describe a woman with whom he wished to have sex. Again, as a woman, this is disgusting for me and for you too, because I mentored you to be neither chauvinistic or misogynistic"

"Well, well, all hail to the wisdom of Ann," James boldly proclaimed as he laughed aloud. "So true are your words and insights, yet I must tell you that most men, when in a group, seem to be ruled by the little head/brain, instead of the bigger head/brain. So from this, come many nasty things that are demeaning to women and this is the reason I shun being around large groups of men, because they have the proclivity to be sexually crude, and quite graphically to wit."

"That being said, many of the men, if not the women, who are outraged at what Donald Trump says are guilty of the exact same thing they are criticizing him for. It's not right, I abhor it, but it is and is, it is. So Hillary Clinton will pound hard on this, all the while ignoring her husband is a world-class sexual predator and quite possibly a pedophile as well."

"Rather than focusing on the indiscretions of Donald Trump or Bill Clinton, we would be better served focusing on solutions of what the populace suffers: high unemployment, illegal immigration and one-sided free trade agreements, like NAFTA and TPP, that annihilate the U.S. economy by destroying industries and eliminating jobs, taken by other countries with lower operating costs for businesses. So for those who say prices on products will increase by reigning in free trade agreements, undoubtedly, that is true. However, the flip side of having full and gainful employment should trump Trump—cheaper prices, which can be more than negated by having more disposable income, from having more employed citizens."

Ann then joined in, praising James for his insights, as he proclaimed, "We also have the presidential candidates of Libertarian, Gary Johnson and Green Party candidate, Dr. Jill Stein—and now in the final countdown of the race, yet another write in candidate surfaces as we are told to "meet" Evan McMullin, the Ex-CIA Operative who is taking Trump votes in Utah."

"I personally gravitate to libertarian principles of a limited government and personal freedom but really have a problem with 'free trade' as I have seen how it has decimated jobs and industries in America. Dr. Stein has some good ideas but history repeats itself and there is no question—socialism will always implode upon itself, as revealed in Dr. Newton's book, *Planet of the Stupids.* Some commentators have pointed out the Green Party is just a new iteration of the Communist Party. This is much more accurate and far less ludicrous than many people will conclude; and you and I both know, James, 'global warming' is a 'global myth', supported by Dr. Stein and the Green Party, whereby the U.N. uses it as a reason to tax us more through a global carbon tax. Me sees the vestiges of Babylon rising from the ashes that should be buried—and the U.N. as well."

"Ha-ha ha-ha," James mockingly laughed in disbelief, "I think we need to circle back to the Trans-Pacific Partnership, which is a trade agreement that will send even more U.S. jobs and industries off shore. President Obama, the illegal alien President, is trying to ram this through congress before his presidential term expires. Let's be very aware Hillary initially favored this trade agreement, but then recanted in an effort to appeal to Bernie Sanders' voters."

"I will also tell everyone who will listen to consider this: the veracity of any Clinton should always be doubted. Remember, Bill Clinton said he would never support a free trade agreement and then rammed NAFTA through the Senate, two years later. So, I would say you can never trust a Clinton, buckaroo, because they are full of pooh and hop around on policy positions like a kangaroo, as it suits their needs to deceive us! As for the, Trumpster, he seems to understand the deleterious effects of free trade and how it destroys the job and industry base in America. It would be warranted to say, if Trump is elected, look for an assassination attempt on him as what happened to Ronald Reagan and John Kennedy, because the Illuminati cult wants free trade and wants open borders, as well.

"Please take a break my Whale Whisperer, since I have something germane to add to the mix, James," Ann pleaded.

"Mix away, share your sway," James mockingly shared with Ann.

"So my sway... my say, James, is about the global open border experiment," Ann sashayed. "Nowhere is Europe, the European Common Market (ECM), or the European Union (EU) has open borders led to anything good. In Switzerland, Africans immigrate and usually become agents of theft and sexual assault, for which they are lightly slapped on the hand in court and released in a few days, only to repeat their crimes. In Germany, the people who are so fed up with emigrees who do not assimilate into their culture and are prone to crime as well are voting against the party of German Prime Minister, Angela Merkel. France has had several terrorist attacks, attributed to foreign immigrants. In the state of Texas in the last ten years, illegal aliens have committed 46.000 violent crimes and rapes. So you see, *mon ami*, free and open borders lead to vastly increased crime and a destabilization of the society having an influx of aliens. This does not even take into account the social costs of educating immigrant children, free medical care and EBT (food stamps). Also there is a growing sentiment in many of the parts of the world, where they want no part of the free trade Kafkaesque experiment, which I am afraid will be characteristic of the nightmarish qualities of Franz Kafka's bizarre world!"

"I was actually astonished when the people of Great Britain voted to leave the European Common Market, in the brexit vote, because the global elite/oligarchs/Illuminati cult were busy using their control of the media outlets to scare people from supporting this sovereignty movement. Everyone predicted the economy of Great Britain would implode; instead it has expanded. Too bad, so sad, in this instance, the illuminati has been had, LMAO!"

"I'm a laughing, not much gaffing, don't intend to be lashing but need to be graphing... a new direction for the citizens of America," James laughed within his words. "Hillary Clinton has presented herself the agent of change because she is a woman and infers she is more compassionate than Donald Trump."

"So for Hillary, does a trail of murders made to look like suicides, consistent perjury regarding the security of email servers, and the selling of favors to gain access to the "wheels of government" show compassion? How can she think the laundering of money or the supporting of free trade that robs our country of jobs and companies reflects any compassion? What about taking huge contributions from Wall Street banks, not to mention brokerages and pharmaceutical companies, or paying women only seventy percent of what men are paid for the same job... how do these have any resemblance to compassion?" How is this deemed as compassionate toward women?

"Sadly, Ann, I am afraid Hillary's enthusiastic supporters will never desert her, no matter how much evidence can be mustered to show she is the one unfit to be president! However, the rest of us should detach ourselves from a state of possible brainwashing and look at what really is—without the rose colored glasses of Dr. Pangloss. And didn't I hear somewhere in the debate debacle that 'The Clintons take care of their friends?"

"Well then," James of the political analyst leanings, let us see whether Trump can get over the compassion hump and take a certain lump (person) and drop it in the dump," said Ann, impressed by her own rhymes. "So Trump has been kicked in the rump for being a misogynist and yet few, if any, women, who have worked for him in the Trump organization shower that label on him. We know he pays women a comparable salary to men for a comparable job; Even though in the last days women miraculously surfaced to complain about Trump, I would question 'why now'? And for that matter, is not the burden of proof on the claimant—so let me query, 'where is the proof?' Trump has been called un-presidential, but would not business experience more than make up for that and even be a superior resume? The man has been called hotheaded; if that was true, tell me how all the huge construction projects built by the Trump Organization came into fruition?

There is the issue of Trump's being derided for having no foreign policy experience, yet neither did Barak Obama… and for all of Hillary's experience in this sphere, can anyone name even one success for her beyond the Iran nuclear agreement, and did that even make the world any safer? Everywhere Hillary goes there appears to be a path of destruction and destabilization, like in Libya and Syria. Trump has been criticized for wanting to complete the building of a wall along the Mexican border as racist, but I contend wanting to control the flow of drugs, terrorists, rapists and murderers is hardly being racist and more akin to a pragmatic solution, that bring more safety and lower social services/welfare costs from the care of illegal aliens, including free medical care."

"And this in some ways is just the short list, James! It is enough, however, to make it difficult to see just how Hillary Clinton could ever 'make our country great again' and much easier to see how Donald Trump might be able to pull this off!"

"Certainly there are some good ideas in the Libertarian Party and their presidential nominee, Gary Johnson, former New Mexico governor, and Dr. Jill Stein," James stated, not wanting to whine. "Getting the government out of the lives of people, eliminating the incarceration of non-violent drug offenders, cutting the U.S. military budget and the legalization of Cannabis could be highly beneficial as we find on Gary Johnson's platform. However, Johnson's support of free trade is very problematic for me."

"Dr. Stein's program to help people through government support shows compassion, but can socialism ever work in the long run since it never has anywhere else on Earth, so far! And, Stein's global warming theory will never hold water, as it were, as revealed in John Hanley's *Dark Winter*. So choices there are, now give me a cigar, don't need to go to a bar and would like to see my country thrive, by far!"

"Now," James continued, "there are things of which humanity must be aware. First, the U.N. is not our friend, despite their assertion to the contrary, since this is the mouthpiece for the Illuminati cult and is ready to implement 'carbon taxes' so they can become the NWO (New World Order) and create a one-world government."

"We both know, Ann, nothing good ever comes from super-large governments so just consider what would happen in a huge government, such as the European Common Market, ruled through myriad bureaucrat issued mandates, not held responsible to either the subject government or the populace and ruled autocratically by the Illuminati cult!"

"Wow, the time is now to have free and fair elections," Ann concluded. "And this must include voter ID, fanatically opposed by President Obama, so we can stop people registering to vote in multiple jurisdictions in the same state and also voting in other states, and also prevent illegal aliens voting in our elections. I even read in the news where a man, long deceased, had just registered to vote, and this brings us back to the illegal voters!"

"Now, look back on our conversation, James, we have covered so much, and yet what change is there? There certainly will be fraudulent voting in the 2016 presidential election... it is just a matter of how much. Is there any alternative to adopting the old voting model of paper ballots, so we can end the manipulation of computerized voting tallies? We have to thank *Judicial Watch*, T*he American Free Press* newspaper, The Pew Poll organization, and Old Dominion University for bringing these voting abuses to light."

"President Obama—who himself was elected, not as the true voice of the people, but by none other than fraudulent voting practices and altered computerized voting tallies—will do everything in his power to continue these sordid practices so as to ensure the election of Hillary Clinton. Our nation must be awakened, James!"

"Well, now, and related to your thoughts, Ann, time to clean the House (and the Senate too) to get rid of the louse," said James quite smugly. "We should know by now career politicians are an anathema to an efficient and honest government. The honest part is almost impossible when there are lobbyists in the legislatures constantly plying their causes and dispensing their favors."

"Most of our legislators in congress spend the bulk of the day, up to six hours I've heard, just working to get money into their political action committees (PACs), at the behest of their parties...

all so they can get re-elected in the next election cycle. *The America Free Press* newspaper has often proposed limiting the terms of congress to one term. While we are at it, should we not consider eliminating the Cadillac health plans and retirement benefits for Congress? Maybe this would eliminate career politicians who living… not feeding at and living off the public trough. Remember my bumper sticker from long ago, Ann, *Clean the House and the Senate too*!"

"So, then, James sans the games, what should we do, what could we do anew?" queried Ann. "Should we pray, who will say hooray, let's bring back the light of God, so that it cuts through the obscuring fog!"

"I will concur with your thoughts, since they are a subject so hot, so when others say not, shows they never have the good fight fought!" James enjoyed the fun and banter that always served as segue between his comments and those Ann made. "May we always abide in the 59th Name of God, Hey Resh Chet… connected to the light, with this we will always be right and never wrong! *Bon jour, mon amour.*"

"*Y a tu tambien, Jaime,* Aleph Kaf Aleph and restore things to their perfect state as per the 7th Name of God," Ann declared. "Remember Illuminati means illumed or enlightened yet the people therein are not!"

"True, *mon amour,* but will my fellow citizens be wise enough to elect the candidate that better serves their interest rather than candidate's own selfish interests and financial gains?"

Pausing before sharing his next thought with Ann, James was finally able to ask her, "Can we even get a clean election with no voting fraud and accurate voting tallies/totals? From the Trust Vote organization, we are most recently apprised that the GEMS vote counting system, used in the five computerized voting systems, including Diebold, can be manipulated very quickly to count one vote for one candidate as much as 25 times and for another candidate, count a vote as little as $1/1000^{th}$ of a tally. This takes cheating to a new level of high tech deceit!"

"Although there are various camps who find Trump God's choice for the election, such as reported by Bob Eschliman in the *Charisma News* magazine, as late as April of 2016, "Donald Trump Is a Central Figure in This Prophecy," I still ask whether Trump has a snow ball's chance in hell of winning the presidency when virtually all the forces of the Illuminati and their minions, including most media outlets and vote counting systems that they control, are combined to prevent his success and focus on his shortcomings while ignoring the career of criminal behavior by Hillary Clinton? This conspiracy against Trump is revealed in bits and pieces as we learn things from Hillary Clinton's hacked emails! We will see, soon enough, *mon ami!*"

"In fact, anticipate a civil disturbance as an outrage manifests from the populace at large, if the election is stolen from Trump. President Obama, who is well experienced in executive orders, could declare martial law and just extend his term indefinitely… which I hear being bandied about by others as fearful of the outcome as we are."

CHAPTER V

LET'S TRANSCEND THE JIVE, THE MENTALITY OF HIVE, AND SEE HOW

WE DO NOT NEED TO ACCEPT LYING, CHEATING, AND THROW IN WIFE BEATING

JAMES QUERIED ANN, "So you think we are done here, do you, *mon amour*? Remember I still have to share with you my experience in a parallel Earth. In my morning meditation, I reached one of those deep levels, where I was able to transcend space and time. I guided myself into a parallel Earth on the fourth dimension and what I found was most gratifying; it completely related to the dysfunctional political environment existing on third-dimension Earth. Now both you and I know, Ann, everything works much better on a higher dimension, rather than a lower one, and the thing that tipped me off was Valery P. Kondratov's, *Geometry of a Uniform Field*, where it becomes obvious each succeeding higher dimension takes on more complex atomic forms or geometries. It is, Ann, the more complex geometries that not only open more creational possibilities but also establish people who live unfettered and also have highly developed psychic abilities. Essentially, any person existing on the fourth-dimension, trying to perpetrate a lie or being deceitful is immediately unmasked since everyone can read the minds of others."

"Ha-ha, ha-ha, LMAO, kind of like you read my mind, right James?" Ann quickly replied!"

James had easily picked up on Ann's banker and enthusiastically replied, "Exactamundo, oh Angelic

One. So, anyway, what I saw on this parallel fourth-dimension Earth was a place where politics were not the slimy affair on my third-dimension Earth. In fact, there were no power hungry or greedy people; no one taking advantage or mistreating their fellow man (or woman). My heart sang, Ann... I saw there a very minimal government, which was Libertarian in orientation, with only the minimum of government services part of the government. There were no restrictions and no zoning laws, since they were unnecessary; career politicians had been replaced with one term, citizen legislators, with no benefits attached to their office. This is so much superior to anything on my third-dimension Earth, than anyone has considered."

"But this is just the beginning of what I saw!" James was enthusiastic as he further shared, "I also went to a fifth-dimension parallel Earth and I really found my dream for third-dimension Earth. What I found was people using an operating system found in Nature and there was literally no government at all. Now you might ask, how the hell could this even work? It is hard to completely explain rather than discussing how Nature itself works. This of course, as you know so well, is covered in Dr. Newton's book, *Beyond the Mists of Time: When Trees Ruled the Earth.* So while the large trees in a forest could hoard all the water and nutrients like carbon and nitrogen and minerals, they share it with the understory trees and plants. The animals, likewise, choose live in harmony, without a government; there is a civil order and animals only kill and eat each other on a natural, and as needed basis. There is no killing for sport and no killing to hoard and store food. Well, this is called anarchy and is always spurned as a state of disorder and yet Nature has shown us an example to follow. I will say no more, other than use your imagination… it could allow us to transcend the limitations of the third-dimension, where Nature manifests this perfection of anarchy."

James' wasn't done yet, desperately trying to convey his passionate beliefs, and saying, "In that humans almost universally think they are superior to the plant kingdom and animals, maybe they should display such in not only their personal actions but those of their governments, as well. The American transcendentalist writers, including Ralph Waldo Emerson and Henry David Thoreau of the *On Walden Pond fame,* celebrated the inner goodness of man, which was more fully manifested as we people immersed ourselves in the actual forces of nature and learn there from."

"*Aleph Kaf Aleph*, or restoring things to their perfect state as the 7th Name of God from *The 72 Names of God* in The Torah in Exodus 14, verses 19-21. On this note I end... for the time being, ha-ha, but I will need your help in the future, my Angelic Ann! 'The Truth is our there,' as *The X-files* TV show often told us. "

"Funny you should mention that, James of the oh, so memorable Whale Whispering fame," Ann laughingly responded, "Because I am sure I will need your counsel, as well. A *bon voyage* of truth for us both! May we stay connected to the light as per the 59th Name of God, Hey Resh Chet!"

ABOUT THE AUTHOR

Dr. Robert J. Newton has lived his life much in the manner he writes... with a quest to surround himself with the highest level knowledge in the myriad areas that ensure we live rich, full lives.

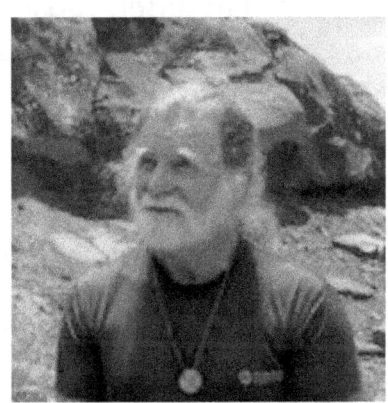

His education has been extensive, ranging from Speech and English at Cal State Fullerton... to a Juris Doctorate from American College of Law, and many certifications in alternative healing. He formalized his career in Naturopathic Medicine as a graduate of Clayton School of Natural Healing.

Newton has lived to serve others; operating an award-winning landscape and design company for many years, as a Christian Science healer for two decades, and more recently as an author, speaker and life and relationship coach. Yoga, Metaphysics,

Spiritual Sciences, Natural Healing, World Religions, Ancient Hermetic teachings… this philosopher and champion for the world has tapped into the roots of spirituality, sexuality, life and love—all with the purpose to enlighten those with a common desire to utilize multiple methods and strategies to approach life more effectively, creatively, radiantly and with great abundance.

Today, Dr. Newton lives his life passionately looking forward… honoring the love and the beliefs he shared with his wife, and writing more novels to plant a "What if" seed in the minds of his readers.

Dr. Newton continues to provide a series of classes and book signings around North and South America, teaching and initiating people into the very things that lead to immortality. A rough outline of this is at www.drrobertnewton.com.

Please feel free to contact Dr. Newton at theta4ia@yahoo.com or at RJNewton@RobertJNewtonAuthor.com for more specifics for these events.

You can also stay connected with him on the following social media platforms:

AMAZON AUTHOR CENTRAL:

http://www.amazon.com/Dr.-Robert-J.-Newton/e/B00LR6A402

WEBSITE(s): http://www.drrobertnewton.com/

http://www.robertjnewtonauthor.com/

TWITTER: https://twitter.com/drrobertjnewton

GOODREADS: https://www.goodreads.com/author/show/6076382.Robert_J_Newton

FACEBOOK:

https://www.facebook.com/robert.newton3

https://www.facebook.com/pages/Dr-Robert-J-Newton-AuthorRadio-Show-Host-Motivational-Speaker/1597130127224474

BLOG: http://www.artistfirst.com/newton.htm

RADIO SHOW:
http://www.artistfirst.com/newton.htm

The Dr. Robert J. Newton Radio Show is a lively discussion of scientific and spiritual subjects, including zero point energy, Zeitgeist (the sharing and sustaining of Earth's resources among all people, not just a few   rich   oligarchs),   and cutting edge healing modalities, as well as powerful mind reprogramming, developing psychic abilities and altered states of consciousness and reality.

Dr. Newton also does motivational speaking, corporate operating strategies, life success and relationship counseling.

Check www.greatmotivationaltalks.com

OTHER BOOKS BY THE AUTHOR

A PROLIFIC WRITER, Dr. Newton brings a wide array of reading to readers who enjoy having their minds challenged in the midst of a good read. Available in various formats: Amazon paperback, Kindle, Barnes and Noble and Ivy's bookstore. He invites readers to...

Take advantage of my invitation to become a part of my VIP Reader community, and get a little taste for some of the other writing that, as non-fiction, addresses many of the same issues discussed throughout this book, but in a little less technical manner.

I am passionate—ever so passionate about the messages I am intended to deliver—and realize there are readers of every vent out there waiting for me to speak (write) in a tone that both challenges their thinking and inspires the possibilities. Join me today...

http://www.robertjnewtonauthor.com/vip-readers/

or head right over to my books page and access them at: http://bit.ly/RNewtonAuthor

The Immortality Prophecy: Let The Reveal Begin (July 2016)

Planet of the Stupids: Bringing Back the Light of God to Planet Earth-With a Paradise Found (March 2016)

In Search of the Body Immortal: Let the Journey Begin (October 2015)

Beyond the Mists of Time: When Trees Ruled the Earth And The State of Balance and Euphoria That Ensued There From (March 2015)

The Hidden Codes of God: A Journey to the Unknown Secrets and Dimensions of the Divine and the Energy of Love (March 2015)

Pathways to God: Experiencing the Energies of the Living God in Your Everyday Life (April, 2012)

A Map to Healing and Your Essential Divinity

Through Theta Consciousness: Physics of the Immortal "Light Body" and the Creator's Template of Perfection and Abundance for His People! (March 2012) Note: This book has an updated version that will be available sometime in November.

REQUEST FOR REVIEWS

IF YOU ENJOYED reading *A Nation of Deceit,* I would appreciate it if you would help others enjoy the book, too.

LEND IT. This book is lending enabled, so please feel free to share with a friend.

RECOMMEND IT. Please help other readers find the book by recommending it to readers' groups, discussion boards, Goodreads, etc.

REVIEW IT. Please tell others why you liked this book by reviewing it on the site where you purchased it, on your favorite book site, or your own blog.

EMAIL ME. I'd love to hear from you. theta4ia@yahoo.com
RJNewton@RobertJNewtonAuthor.com

www.ingramcontent.com/pod-product-compliance
Lightning Source LLC
Chambersburg PA
CBHW060118260626
47160CB00005B/1928

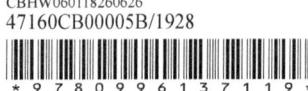